THE ROOKIE

CATHRYN FOX

ISBN Ebook: 978-1-989374-41-2

ISBN Print: 978-1-989374-40-5

WES

I lift my head to the sound of seagulls squawking over the Bay of Fundy and breathe in the briny, ocean air. I've been on the road with the Seattle Shooters for the past hockey season and while I love what I do—I live to play the game—sometimes a guy just needs to return to his roots to center himself.

I take in the picturesque scenery before me, the fishing vessels bobbing in the rising tide, and the numerous tourists who flock to Nova Scotia every year for the scenic charm, friendly people, and of course, the catch of the day—which reminds me why I'm standing at the docks in the first place.

I tug my ballcap down on my head and walk to the Lobster Pound. The huge red building near the docks has been around for as long as I can remember. It's one of many places dotting the shoreline that sell fresh and canned lobster, as well as other products, and supply our orchard with lobster shells. We compost the shells to feed the fruit trees on our family farm. Nothing goes to waste in our neck of the woods.

I swing open the door, a little bell jingling overhead as the air conditioning hits like a refreshing wave, cooling the droplets on my forehead. The smell of seafood fills my nostrils as my gaze goes to the guy at the back of the shop. He's dressed in coveralls, a ball cap, and steel-toed boots. His back is to me as he takes lobster from a gray bin and places them in a big, gurgling tank. I shove my hands into my pockets and size up the fillets creatively arranged on crushed ice in the seafood display counter before me, as I wait for him to finish his task.

After a couple minutes pass and he reaches for another bin, I call out to him, assuming he hadn't heard me come in. "Hey Mack," I say. "I'm here to pick up the shells for the Hatfield farm." I have no idea what the guy's name is, but Mack is just a friendly moniker we call someone when we don't know their name.

The guy straightens, and turns to me. That's when I realize my mistake. Not a guy. Nope, not a guy at all. Just a girl dressed in clothes that made me think she was of a different gender. I'm used to the puck bunnies, and their tight, flimsy designer clothes. The woman before me is the anthesis of those women, and I'm not saying that's a bad thing.

"Oh, I didn't hear—" Her big eyes narrow in on me, and what I only assume was the beginning of a smile morphs into a scowl. It hits like a puck to the face, and I nearly falter backwards.

Okay, I get it. She doesn't like being called Mack. I hold my hands up, palms out. "Sorry...I thought—"

"Your shells are over there," she says and points to a big gray bin beside the door. My apology clings to my tongue as she goes back to what she was doing, completely dismissing me.

Alrighty then. "Thanks," I say, even though I'm sure she's no longer listening to me, but I'm a simple farm boy who was raised with manners, and can't help myself. I'm about to grab the shells and leave when she mumbles something under her breath. Something that sounds like asshole. What the hell?

"Do I know you?"

"You tell me," she counters, and drops the last of the lobsters into the big tank. She tugs off yellow gloves, and sets them in a nearby sink. I wrack my brain. We've been picking up shells from the Baxter family for years. It's always been a family run business and if memory serves me correctly, there are four girls in the family, and they've all been helping out at the pound since they could walk. She's obviously one of them, but not one I used to see regularly.

Her head lifts and I take in her pretty profile, and that's when recognition hits. "Charlotte?"

She snorts, and shakes her head. "Don't you mean, Charlie?"

Okay, now I'm confused. Was there a Charlotte and a Charlie and I'm mixing them up? Wait, isn't Charlie short for Charlotte? I don't know, but what I do know is that the Charlotte I remember was a few years younger than me. We very rarely crossed paths here at the pound, but I'd see her when she was leaving U15 hockey practice and I was gearing up for my U18 game. She was one hell of a player, and I used to enjoy watching the team's highest scorer. I scratch my head, not sure what I ever did to her—I don't even remember speaking to her—but it's clear from her scowl that she doesn't like me much.

She folds her arms and aims those gorgeous blue eyes at me. "Is there anything else you need, Wes?"

I blink at her. "You know me?"

"Of course, I know you," she huffs out. "Everyone knows you. You're Weston Hatfield, a famous hockey player. You put Digby, Nova Scotia, on the map."

"It's just Wes. I don't go by Weston." Not that there is anything wrong with the name—it was, after all, my grandfather's name—but I just prefer Wes.

"Fine, Wes." She takes her ballcap off, and bends forward to shake out her long blonde hair. My gaze goes to the sexy bend of her body, the way her overalls hug her curves, not to mention the sweet swell of her ass. As I stare, unable to tear my gaze away, I realize one of two things are happening. Either my jeans shrank in the laundry last night, or I really like the vision before me. She pulls an elastic off her wrist to tie her long hair into a ponytail. My heart beats a little faster against my ribs as she straightens and looks back at me.

"You're still here?"

My dry throat scratches as I work to swallow. Despite what's written and rumored about me, it's been a while since I've been with a girl. I'm the new guy on the team, the rookie, and my first season was spent proving myself. I didn't have a lot of time for extracurricular activities, no matter what was said. Now that the season is over, however... That thought brings on a laugh. Am I really thinking about starting something with a girl who clearly hates me—for reasons I don't understand? Plus, lessons learned taught me the girls in this town are always looking for a way out. I'm not about to make the mistake of getting involved with anyone from here, only to get dumped when something bigger and better comes along. Not again, anyway.

A line forms on her forehead as she frowns at me. "Something funny?"

"No...I just ah...I don't mean to sound stupid, but are you or aren't you Charlotte from U15 hockey."

"Of course I am."

"You go by Charlie now?"

The cute freckles around her nose bunch as her lips pinch, and one hip juts out as she plants her hand on it in a no-nonsense manner. Nothing about her clothes, or the way she's standing there glaring at me should be construed as sexy. It's not the look she's going for. She's not trying to impress me by any means, which means my damn dick should not be hardening.

Down boy.

"You say that like you had nothing to do with it," she shoots back, blatant accusation dripping from her words.

My head rears back. "What are you talking about?" I barely know her. Why would I have anything to do with her nickname?

She looks like she's about to explain it, but then she exhales and says, "You won, it's Charlie."

I have no idea what I won, but I say, "It suits you."

She glances at her clothes. "Yeah, of course you'd say that." Before I can ask what the hell she means, the door opens and in walks a group of tourists, no doubt from the big bus that just pulled up. She calls for help from the back room, and when a girl with very similar features to Charlie's jumps in to help, Charlie turns her attention to the people stepping up to the counter. A smile reserved for tourists—or people she likes —lights up her pretty face.

I stand there for a second, a little mesmerized by her beauty as she chats easily with all the sightseers. She hoists a new bin of lobsters up to the counter for her customers to peruse, and for a tiny girl, she's damn strong. That bin must weigh a good fifty pounds. It's probably half her weight.

I get shuffled to the back of the store as more customers pile in, everyone looking for fresh lobster and scallops, and I scoop up the bin with the lobster shells and step out into the fresh afternoon air.

My phone pings and I walk to the wharf to avoid a group of tourists steamrolling my way and pull it from my pocket. I grin as I read the text from Rider, letting me know his arrival time. He and Jules are flying here from Seattle and I'm looking forward to showing them around my province. They're leaving their little girl Sophie with Jules' family and are taking a much-needed adult vacation. I text him back to let him know I'll be at the airport to pick them up first thing tomorrow.

I shove my phone back into my pocket, and lift my head at the sound of papers flapping in the ocean breeze. I spot flyers in a wooden box nailed to the end of the dock, and pull one out to read about the boating and whale watching tours to Brier Island. It's funny. I lived here until I went off to college and I've never once went on a tour or camped at Brier Island. I scan the brochure and check the departure dates for the overnight trip. I have no doubt Jules and Rider would love to do something like this.

"You won't enjoy it."

I turn to find Charlie coming my way, and as I take in the way her breasts tent the bib of her coveralls, and the soft sway of her hips as she walks, my dick twitches, once again reminding me I haven't been with anyone in a long time. Charlie here though, she's different from the girls who hang out at the rink and pretend they're not cold in their skimpy clothes, even though hypothermia is nipping at their heels. Charlie would likely show up in an ankle length coat, a toque, and mittens. Something tells me she's smart like that.

"What makes you say that?" I ask as she walks past me, and with deft fingers unties a boat from the metal ring attached to the dock like she's done it a million times before. Rope in hand, and with the grace of a seasoned fisherman, she jumps onto the lobster boat and lands with a loud thud.

"Your legs." She efficiently weaves the rope around a metal post attached to the floor of the vessel. It probably has a fancy boat name, but I'm a farm boy, not a fisherman, so I don't know it.

"What about them?" I ask.

"Those aren't sea legs." I glance at my legs and when I look back at her, I'm pretty sure she's trying to hold back a grin. For a split second, I think she might be flirting with me. "Legs like those, they'll have you tripping up and before you know it, you'll be losing your lunch over the side of the boat."

"Are you messing with me?" She steps into the cab, and starts the boat. I watch as she expertly handles the large craft like it's an extension of her small body. "What are you doing? Should you be on that thing alone?" I glance around. "Shouldn't you get the captain? Is he around here? I can get him for you."

"I'm a boat-napper, and I work alone." She puts her fingers to her lips to hush me and I get it, my question was judgmental and sexist. I really didn't mean it that way. I'm truly impressed with her skills. "Tell no one."

I laugh, and so does she, but I don't think she's laughing with me. She spins the big wheel and moves away from the dock, and even though I suspect she's laughing *at* me and my stupid questions, I stand there, a big ridiculous grin on my face as I watch her go. I glance at the brochure again, more intrigued than I was moments ago. The engine revs and I shade the sun from my eyes and look past the dock.

"Where are you going?" I shout out.

"Anywhere but here."

I nod. I get it. She wants out of rural Nova Scotia, like every other person our age. Fishing and farming aren't for everyone. I wave the brochure at her. "Do you run these tours?"

"Of course not. That would be a man's job."

Okay, another stupid question, and another sarcastic response I deserve. But I like it. She's non-apologetic, seems completely comfortable with who she is and what she does, and she can handle a big-ass boat all by herself. There's something so damn real about her, it taunts me—draws me in.

Before I can call her on her lie, she shakes her head. "Don't do it, Wes," she yells back at me, her words barely audible over the roar of the engine.

"I'm doing it, Captain," I holler back, and as she shakes her head, I can't deny that I might want to 'do it' with her. Might?

Yeah, okay. I for sure want to 'do it' with her, despite the fact that she hates me. But nothing about getting involved with Charlie—a local girl more likely than not looking for a ticket out of rural Nova Scotia—is smart or wise, and I usually like to listen to that smart, inner voice and make informed decisions.

Screw that, Mack.

2

CHARLIE

If you think I was flirting with him, I wasn't. I was simply trying to engage in polite conversation, doing the best a girl can do when she only has one working brain cell. Apparently, all the others packed a bag and headed south the second Weston—or rather Wes—Hatfield stepped into the Lobster Pound. I heard he was back in town, and figured sooner or later I'd run into him. We do, after all, provide his farm with lobster shells on a regular basis. I just hadn't expected my far too needy body to react quite the way it had when he strolled into the shop with pants that fit too nicely, and a T-shirt that did little to hide rippling ab muscles. I hate the boy who relentlessly teased me the winter before I grew boobs.

My God, it's been a little over twenty-four hours since I set eyes on his gorgeous face, and lean muscled body, and I'm pretty sure my nipples are still hard enough to shuck scallops —now that would be a sight to see for the upcoming shucking competition. Nevertheless, I might not like him, but that doesn't mean I don't know a hot guy when I see one.

Seriously, though. I hope he takes my advice and doesn't sign up for a tour. I must check on my online reservation system. We're all booked except for this coming weekend. If he doesn't jump on it, he likely won't get it, and I'd rather go a weekend without income than spend it with him.

Spending hours on a boat with him, our bodies in close proximity with no way to escape, would be pure torture and might just send my body into hyperdrive. The last thing I want is for the cocky hockey player who teased me at the rink to know I'm attracted to him. I mean, did you see his face, acting all innocent, like he hadn't tormented me about my non-existent curves, or breasts, calling me Charlie instead of Charlotte and rudely joking that I must have signed up for the girls' team by mistake. The nickname eventually stuck and I don't hate it, but that doesn't mean he's not the world's biggest asshole, either.

Thank God we were never in the same school. He's older than me by three years, so by the time I'd reached high school, he was off to college, and up until yesterday I was able to avoid him by running the other way when I saw him coming, or ducking into the back office when his folks sent him to pick up the lobster shells.

I shove the last of the brochures into my bag and turn the sign on the door from open to close. The warm night air falls over me as I make my way along the shore to restock the shelves with my tour pamphlets. It's a side hustle I started last summer. With lobster season finished until the fall, I repurposed the boat for whale-watching tours. I'm an entrepreneur at heart, and I have great management skills, if I do say so myself. That's why I went to the city for a four-year degree in business management, which I've not really put to use outside my hometown. A measure of guilt eats at me. The truth is, I love it here in rural Nova Scotia. I love working the fishing boat with my sisters as well as the salty fishermen we hire to help out. Dad left after his fourth daughter was born, leaving Mom, and me, since I was seven, and the oldest, to run the show ourselves.

I guess seven years into the marriage he decided this life wasn't for him. He wanted different things, but lobster fishing is in my mother's blood and according to her, the only thing she was good at. She's a fifth-generation seafarer, and my father wanted her to walk away from it—wanted her to be something she wasn't.

I walk along the shore, contentment weaving its way through my blood as seagulls circle above, looking for a late day snack. I breathe in the thick, salted air, and I get why Mom couldn't leave. I love it here too, but I have a degree she paid for, and I don't want it to go to waste. She's making sure all of us girls get our education, and really, she doesn't need any of us to help her with the business. She can hire out like any other company, and she's wanted to make sure she gave us opportunities, because she never wanted to keep us here for fear that we'd come to resent it—like our father.

The sea isn't in everyone's soul.

While it is in mine, there's guilt too. Mom worked hard to make sure I was educated, and I can't let that money go to waste, which is why I applied for a couple of jobs in Toronto last month, and I really shouldn't be hoping they fall through. But she knows I'm good at other things besides deep sea fishing, and wants me to explore my opportunities.

The sea isn't going anywhere, luv.

I grin as her words dance in my brain, and music blares from the open windows at Captain Jack's Fish Shack. I cut down the path, and pull open the glass door, and the smell of deep-fried food reaches my nostrils. They do make the best fish and chips around and my stomach grumbles, reminding me I'd skipped lunch today. The tourist season is picking up, and while that's good for the bottom line, I barely had time to breathe.

I reach into my bag and pull out a handful of brochures as I spin the rack with my other hand, to see how many of my old fliers are left. A loud booming voice reaches my ears and my entire body reacts in ways I wish it wouldn't.

Wes Hatfield.

Really? Wes is here? At Captain Jack's? Does this mean I'm going to run into the big jerk everywhere I go? I grip the metal rack to stop it from spinning, and slowly, carefully, glance around the display, but the second I do, I wish I hadn't. As if sensing my eyes on him, Wes' head lifts, and those light brown eyes latch on mine. Damn. Damn. Damn. I jump back to hide, but it's too late for that. Too late to pretend I wasn't checking him out, even though I wasn't—I don't think—and I have nothing to feel guilty about, so I have no idea why I'm trying to make myself invisible.

I shake my head at my foolishness, and as I pull myself together, I recklessly start jamming brochures into the slot. A strong wave of perfume wafts before my nose as Breton Boudreau, Wes Hatfield's high school girlfriend walks by, a coffee carafe in her hand. I'm surprised she's still here. Those who don't join the family business leave right after high school. My friends are all long gone, and of course, none of the people I met at college are working in this podunk town.

I keep my head down, but I can still feel Wes' eyes on me. From my peripheral vision, I spot Breton walking to his table, an extra little sway to her hips when she approaches. I almost snort. Maybe she's trying to get him back. It's not like she has any competition.

Taking my time, I clean up the rack, and I'm not lingering because I want to eavesdrop. That's not my style. I'm taking my time because I made a mess of the arrangement, and I want my brochures to stand out. If there is one thing I love, it's being on the boat, touring the bay for whales, or hiking Brier Island.

Once I'm done shuffling, I stand back and admire my handiwork. I'm pleased with the brochures I made weeks ago, and love how the color pops and grabs attention. Ready to move on to the next restaurant, I hike my bag up higher on my shoulder, and I'm about to turn when a big heavy palm lands on my shoulder.

The heat of his skin scorches my body and travels downward, creating warmth and need in every erogenous zone along the way. Oh boy.

"Hey," a deep male voice says, and I don't need to turn to know that big hand belongs to Wes.

Keep your cool, Charlie.

Do not act like you want to throw yourself at him and beg him to take you, right here, on the restaurant floor. I take a fast breath and move forward until his hand falls from my shoulder. With my lips pinched tight, I turn to face him, but what I failed to do was brace myself against that small smile flirting with those ridiculous kissable lips.

"What?" I blurt out, flustered, aroused...confused at the things this man makes me feel.

He holds his hand up, the same one that left a burning imprint on my shoulder. "Sorry, I didn't mean to grab you like that." He looks over his shoulder and rubs his chin. Why the hell is he acting so cagey? Wes Hatfield isn't as calm and cool as he's trying to portray. How interesting.

"What *did* you mean, then?"

His laugh is nervous, forced, and he takes a small step closer. The smell of deep-fried food is replaced with the enticing aroma of freshly washed skin, and laundered clothes. I think he uses the same fabric softener as I do. Ohmigod, why the hell am I thinking about fabric softener when he's standing so close, crowding me...arousing me?

I clear my throat and step back a bit, needing a reprieve from his gravitational force, but he follows me, keeping close. Electricity arcs between our bodies, but I'm sure I'm the only one feeling it. I might have grown boobs and hips, but they're certainly not noticeable beneath my loose-fitting T-shirt and jeans, and from the women I've seen on this man's arms—our local paper always follows their homegrown hero—I am so not his type.

Another little nervous laugh bubbles in his throat, and he glances over his shoulders a third time. I lean to the side to see what's ruffling his feathers, and I spot Breton standing at his table, her eyes narrowed, brimming with shock and disbelief, as she stares at us.

"What's going—"

He puts his hands on my shoulders again and I forget what I was going to say next. "Please, just go with this. I'll explain everything later."

I open my mouth again, and his lips land on mine. Wait, what the hell does he think he doing? That wasn't a damn invitation… Oh, hey, wow, that's kind of nice. Soft. Sweet. Hmm, he tastes like warm rum, and I could use a glass or ten at the moment. That's probably the reason I'm sliding my arms around his body, widening my fingers so I can touch every inch of his hardness. Yeah, yeah, that has to be it. Nothing else makes sense. I don't even like this guy. His fingers on my shoulders tighten, and that's when I realize my eyes are shut. I open them to find light brown eyes that can only be described as salted caramel staring back. Our mouths hang out a little longer, our lips a breath apart, as he whispers to me.

"Thank you."

"What?"

"For pretending…."

Pretending? What the hell is he talking about?

"Can you please do it for a second longer?" he asks. "I know it's a lot to ask, but…"

"Sure," I say, my voice a breathless whisper. I part my lips without hesitation, ready to kiss him a second longer, or maybe even an hour, when his deep voice curls around me.

"I really appreciate it."

With my 'good-decision-making-skills' on hiatus, it's hard to understand what he's saying to me. Cripes, I don't really believe in fairy tales or happily ever after, but I feel like Cinderella with birds chirping and singing as they fly and dance around my head. "Appreciate it?"

"Yeah, the pretending...you...me..." His dark lashes fall slowly over those rich, caramel eyes. "This is for show." He gestures with a nod toward Breton, and that's when that one working brain cell I have left smacks some sense into me.

I straighten and square my shoulders. "Yeah, sure. I know."

Nope, didn't know. Still kind of don't know what's going on.

"I'll pay you back for this. I promise." He tugs on my hand to set me into motion. The room is wobbly in my view, and I can't seem to focus on anything. Like a fish following a shiny lure, I blindly let him lead me to his table and he holds his hand out for me to slide in. I drop down and shimmy to the other side, thankful to be off my feet for a second.

I smile at the two people seated across from me, and instantly recognize Rider Lewis, aka The Wingman. The gorgeous woman with him must be his wife. Breton is saying something—correction, sputtering and spitting something— and my gaze slowly turns her way. Why do I feel like I'm caught in a bad nightmare, and everything is moving in slow motion?

"...You have got to be kidding me," Breton says, and the strangers seated across from me squirm uncomfortably, but Wes here, he throws his arm around me, and tugs me closer. I shouldn't like the way my body presses against his, nor should I like the strength in his embrace, and the need it arouses in me. His fingers skate over my skin, and in no way at all should that reduce me to a ridiculous schoolgirl crushing on the popular jock. I never did that back in high school, and have no intentions of losing myself, or who I really am, in this guy. Which means I need to get the hell out of here, pronto.

His hand slides up and he lightly brushes my cheek. I lean into him, absorbing his warmth. Okay, what was that I just told myself?

"She...she plays for the other team, Wes," Breton blurts out, and heat crawls into my face as her words register. I've never once corrected the rumor, never cared too. If people want to think I prefer girls over guys, let them.

Wes' hand tightens for a second and then he laughs it off. "Small towns and their rumor mills." He winks at me. "Maybe I'm glad there were rumors. Otherwise, some other guy might have snatched this beautiful woman up before I found my way back home."

I smile at him, and my lust-rattled brain slowly starts to put the pieces together—he wants me to pretend to be his girl-friend. I'm not sure why. Maybe it's some weird revenge scheme against his ex, or some ploy to make her jealous and win her back, and I just happened to be at the right place at the right time for him. Or the wrong place at the wrong time. Yeah, that's more like it.

"You know I can't stay long, babe," I say, falling into the ridiculous role, for reasons I can't explain. "I still have some work to do."

"We were just about to order dessert. You can stay for dessert, can't you? You know they make the best apple pie here."

"I...I..."

"Please," he murmurs quietly as Breton stomps off. "It's the least I can do, you know, for letting me kiss you like that." He stares at me with those syrupy eyes, and as my heart beats faster, I'm suddenly back in fairy tale land, breathing in a bed of daisy's as I run barefoot through the wide-open meadow, the sun in my hair, the birds singing a love....

Ohmigod, kill me now.

"I suppose," I say. What the hell am I doing? What happened to that no-nonsense woman who promised herself she'd never get drawn in by a charming guy? Then again, I'm a bit of a softie when it comes right down to it, always the first to jump in when someone needs help, which clearly Wes needs. Is it really going to hurt me to have a piece of pie with him and his friends—payment for letting him kiss me? Afterward, I can simply go out of my way to avoid him, but pie for payment, yeah, why not? And no, I am not going to be thinking that I should be the one rewarding him somehow because that kiss was...traumatizing in the most delicious ways that are going to keep me up at night.

"You're welcome," I say, the fight going out of me.

"I appreciate that you didn't stab me in the nuts with a fork when I kissed you."

"Only because I didn't have one in my hand," I lie. I liked it. A lot.

He grins and his friends burst out laughing. "So if I ever do that again, I'll be sure not—"

"We won't be doing that again."

His brow crinkles. "That bad, huh?"

There's a hint of teasing in his voice but I also sense he's fishing for information. He can't seriously think he's a bad kisser. Can't seriously be hoping I liked it. Which, of course, I did.

"Uh huh."

"Yeah, well I appreciate you helping me out." He glances at Breton, then briefly looks down, a frown on his face, and I can't help but think he's remembering something painful. "I can't…"

Breton hurt him. I hate that. I hate seeing anyone hurting. Yeah, I know he was mean to me, but still…

I smile at his friends as he struggles with some internal war. "Nice to meet you both. Rider, I'm a fan."

His smile is big and genuine, and there is a real warmth about him as he extends his hand to shake my hand. "Thanks. This is my wife, Jules."

"They're visiting from Seattle," Wes tells me like he's back on his game.

"Nice, I hope you enjoy your stay. How long are you here?"

"For a week."

"I suppose I'll see you around then." It's Wes I'm avoiding, not these two.

"Yeah, you will be," Jules says a big smile on her face. "We just went online and booked a tour on your boat. We can't wait. We're so excited to go whale watching and camping. Aren't we, Rider?"

"You bet."

"Great," I say through clenched teeth as I force a smile and remind myself to bring along a short plank. You know, so I can take a nice long walk off it.

FML.

"Hey Mack," I joke, and cringe as my voice comes out a little deeper than I intended. But come on, how am I not supposed to sound aroused as I watch Charlie on her boat, down on her hands and knees, scrubbing at something that looks like gum from the deck. There isn't any other girl in the world who could make that sexy.

Her head lifts and she blows a long strand of blonde hair from her eyes as they glare at me. "I'm kidding, I'm kidding," I say. "I knew it was you down there."

"You sure about that?"

"Charlie Baxter, you're one of a kind and hard to miss." Staring at me like she's not sure if that's a compliment or not, I add, "That's a good thing, trust me, and I come in peace." She continues to glare, clearly suspicious, but then her eyes narrow when her gaze drops to take in the two ice cream cones in my hand.

"What are you doing here?" she asks, and wipes her brow with her arm, but honestly, she couldn't look any more adorable if she tried.

I hold one cone out to her. "I brought ice cream."

She stands and drops a rag into a bucket. "Why did you do that?"

I shrug. "I don't know. It's a hot afternoon, and I saw you here after we walked the beach and thought you might like an ice cream. You do like ice cream, don't you?"

"Of course, I do." She takes off her yellow gloves, drapes them over the side of the bucket, and I wonder how many pairs she has of those things. "That was nice of you."

"Imagine that. Me, nice."

"Did it hurt much?" Before I can answer, she effortlessly jumps from the boat to the dock, and I hand her the chocolate cone. Hair sticks to her forehead as she angles her head. "How did you know I liked chocolate?"

"Who doesn't like chocolate, Charlie?"

"If you're trying to make up for that dreadful kiss, the pie was enough."

"I wasn't. The ice cream had nothing to do with the kiss." I stand there and whistle innocently, like I'm not up to something else. But I am.

She exhales loudly and asks, "What now?"

I nod my head toward Jules and Rider as they walk the rocky beach, stopping to pick up shells. "We're headed into the city for a couple hours. Jules had no idea we'd be going whale watching or hiking or camping." I laugh. "I didn't either, until I saw your brochures."

"Lucky me."

"What was that?" I ask.

"Nothing."

She has a less than impressed look on her face, so I continue with. "Jules really likes you. She obviously has good taste."

"Stop complimenting and tell me what you want."

Okay, I like a girl who gets straight to the point. "She was wondering if you'd like to join us. We're headed to The Trail Shop in the city and she figured since you do the tours, you'd know what gear she'd need to pick up."

Charlie glances over at Jules, who waves to her. Charlie smiles, and I sense a deep loneliness about her, a sadness that I instantly want to soothe. Have all her friends left for bigger and better too?

"You don't have to if you don't want," I explain. "It won't hurt her feelings. She'll understand if you're busy."

She takes a lick of her dripping ice cream cone, and glances out at the ocean. I'm not sure what's going through her head, but she stares at the waves for a long time. I lick my ice cream and for a second think she might have forgotten I was standing there.

She spins, and nods. "Okay, I can go. There's a few things I need to pick up anyway." She glances at her clothes. "What time are you leaving? I'd like to get showered and changed first."

"You don't need to change." My gaze drops to take in her frayed jean shorts and raggedy, threadbare, Rolling Stones T-shirt. I stifle a moan of pleasure that's trying to rise in my throat. My smile however, I can't seem to wipe that from my face. "You look great. I'm in shorts, too."

"You're in nice khaki shorts, and *you're* the one who looks great. Not me." She tugs on the frayed end of her shorts. "I'm not going shopping with Jules dressed like this."

I jerk my thumb over my shoulder. "I can give you a ride to your place."

"It's not far. I can walk."

"Or I can drive you."

One hand goes to her hip. "Pushy. Not a great trait, Wes."

I grin. "Stubborn. Not a great trait, Charlie."

"I guess it's a good thing we're not trying to impress each other, then."

I laugh, because dammit, this woman is seriously impressive. "Yeah, because it would be awful if we had to kiss again."

She makes a sound, like she'd eaten something distasteful. "I can't think of anything worse."

I laugh again. I like her. "Are we going to stand here and insult each other for the rest of the day or are you going to let me drive you to your place to get changed?"

"Wait, did you just call me stub—"

"Are you accepting my offer to drive you?" I grin as her eyes narrow in on me, knowing the point goes to me if she refuses.

"Yes, but only because I don't want to keep your friends waiting, and to prove I'm not stubborn."

I hold my hand out and point to my car, not believing for one second that this woman isn't stubborn. But that's not a bad thing. She's an independent girl who knows what she wants, and I like that about her.

I wave Jules and Rider over and they hop into the back seat. Charlie hesitates. "I can sit in the back."

"And you can sit in the front," I say to her over the roof.

She opens her mouth and when I grin at her, she grumbles something and slides into the passenger seat.

"Charlie, I really appreciate you coming along. It's nice to have a girl to shop with," Jules says, and I smile at her in the rearview mirror.

"Happy to do it," Charlie says. "How are you liking Nova Scotia so far?"

"It's beautiful. Quiet, but beautiful. Next time we come back, Sophie will be old enough for us to bring her."

Charlie smiles at the mention of Jules's daughter. Does she want kids of her own? I do, eventually. I've been so busy working toward an NHL career I've not given it much thought, though. I drive her to her house, and she invites us to wait inside while she gets changed. We step into the big old homestead, and she calls out to her mother.

Mrs. Baxter comes around the corner, a smile on her face when she sees me.

"Wes, it's so great to see you," she says, holding her arms out for a hug. I lean in and hug her, and her smile widens when she sees Rider and Jules behind me. Her hands go to her cheeks. "Oh my, you're Rider Lewis."

"The one and only," he teases, and Jules rolls her eyes at him. "This is my wife, Jules."

"Mom, I'm going to grab a quick shower," Charlie says after the introductions. "Then we're headed to the city for some shopping. Jules didn't pack for boating, so I'm going to help her pick out some things."

"What fun," Mrs. Baxter says.

Charlie rushes up the stairs, and I can't help but stare after her, my eyes on her cute little backside.

"Come in, come in," Mrs. Baxter says, and I tear my gaze away, hoping she hadn't noticed the way I was drooling over her daughter. She walks down the hall and gestures for us to follow. I take my time walking, lagging behind to study the pictures decorating the walls. As an only child, I sort of envy her. I've always wanted brothers and sisters. My cousin Lester, named after his grandfather as well, stayed with us one winter, but I spent a lot of my weekends at hockey camp, and did a month-long stint out west, while he took my spot on the local team and joined in the practices. His parents thought getting him out of the city for a bit would smarten him up and get him on the right track.

I grin as I take in the smiling faces and it's easy to pick out Charlie in the childhood photos. While she's a very down to earth girl, there's a dreamy look on her face in her pictures. What kind of dreams does Charlie Baxter have, and do they take her away from this tourist fishing town?

We sit at the big oaken table, and Mrs. Baxter pours us lemonade. Just then Jules' phone rings and she holds it up. "If you'll excuse me, it's my sister and she's looking after our daughter." She disappears into the other room, and Mrs. Baxter sits with us. Using my thumb, I swipe at the condensation beading on my glass as she dives right into hockey, and I just laugh. Jules comes back into the room and Rider shoots her a questioning glance.

"Everything is good," she says. "Sophie has a slight fever, but she's teething and I'm pretty sure that's all it is."

"Jules is a nurse," I explain, and Mrs. Baxter smiles at her, but then her smile falters.

"My youngest, she's in high school. I think she'd be a great nurse, but she says she prefers to work the boats."

"Really?" I ask, a bit surprised by that. Everyone I grew up with wanted out of this small fishing town.

"She's smart as a whip." She makes a clicking sound with her tongue and points to her head. "And the world needs more nurses."

I take a big drink of sweet lemonade. "You don't want her to stay here and join the family business?"

"I just want her to be happy. I want all my girls to have life experiences, and then decide what's right for them. It can take time to figure out who you are and what you want."

"What about Charlie?" I ask, curious about the tough girl who I'd mistaken for a guy. Breton was quick to point out that Charlie wasn't interested in men, and maybe she's right. I don't mean to sound cocky here, but women sort of like me. They throw themselves at us players all the time. Charlie seems like she'd rather throw some*thing* at me. But each to their own right. Love is love, and who she loves is her business.

"Charlie, well she..." Her head lifts at the shuffling sound behind me. "I want her to be happy."

I study her for a second, and sense she wanted to say something else entirely, but decided against it. I turn and nearly bite off my tongue as Charlie comes down the hall, the fresh fruity scent of her showered skin reaching my nostrils. Face free of makeup and hair tied back, looking exactly like the girl next door—a girl who is out of this farm boy's league— she bounces into the kitchen dressed in a pair of black cotton shorts that tie at the waist and a lightweight blouse with the top two buttons undone.

"Don't you look lovely," her mother says.

She drops a kiss onto her mother's cheek and it's easy to see how much they adore one another.

"That was fast," I comment.

She smiles. "Low maintenance. Are we all ready to go?"

"Thanks for the lemonade," I say as Rider stands and helps Mrs. Baxter take our glasses to the sink.

"Come by anytime," she calls out. "Maybe we can all have a barbecue. We're all hockey fans in this house, and I'm sure my daughters would love to meet you, Rider, and Wes, they're going to love to see you again."

Charlie touches her mother's arm lovingly. "I'm sure they're too busy for that, Mom, and Jules and Rider are only here for a week."

"Not too busy for a barbecue," I tell her. Jules and Rider agree, and Charlie glares at me. "What?" I ask. "I'm a growing boy. I need food."

"You need something," she mumbles, and I grin as we all head back outside, and pile into the car. She slides in next to me, and once again her sweet scent fills my senses. I start the car, and we chat about the weather. Conversation eventually turns to Jules' and Rider's Vegas wedding and all the antics that took place, which Charlie loves hearing about. Eventually Jules turns the conversation to Charlie, and Charlie tells us all about the boats, and what it's like being on them with all the rough and gruff fishermen. I'm about to ask more when Charlie redirects to me.

"What was it like growing up on a farm?" she asks, and I get the sense she doesn't like talking about herself much.

"Dirty," I say. "I was always, very, very dirty, and I had to learn to be handy."

I notice the slight change in her breathing, the way the buttons on her blouse rise and fall as she takes in a breath. What, does she like the idea of me being dirty, handy...in a very different way? My thoughts instantly go south, and my dick twitches as I visualize all the ways I could get dirty with this gorgeous woman. My friends fall silent in the back seat as heat arcs between Charlie and me. Moisture dots my forehead and I lean forward to jack the air conditioning, but it does nothing to help cool the flames licking through my veins. Charlie's throat makes a rough sound as she swallows, and the pulse at the base of my throat beats a little faster.

"I don't think we've booked enough time here to see everything," Jules says, cutting through the tension as it builds, and takes up space between Charlie and me.

"At least you'll get to see the Halifax waterfront today. We have to drive by it on the way to The Trail Shop," Charlie says, her voice light and casual. Heck, maybe I'm reading her all wrong. Maybe I'm the only one with inappropriate thoughts, and it's wishful thinking on my part that she has them, too. This could be all in my head and maybe Breton was right. Charlie didn't correct her when she told me my 'girlfriend' played for the other team. As my brain races, Charlie adds, "It's one of my favorite places to explore."

"What do you like best about it?" I ask. It's one of my favorite places too. No matter where I go or live, the east coast will always be in my blood and now that I'm home, I realize just how much I've missed it. I really need to make more time to come back. That thought makes me laugh because most of my friends hate returning home. They find the country life boring. I find it relaxing.

"The atmosphere," she says and exhales. "All the people, the outdoor patios, the ice cream shops. There's a great energy about the city. Probably something to do with the east coast. I used to walk the waterfront almost every day."

"Really?" I reach the city limits and head toward the downtown core. "It's a long way from home."

She shrugs. "Not when I was living in the city."

I turn to look at her, take in her profile as she stares at the curvy road before us. "How long ago was that?"

"A couple years ago. I went to Dalhousie University. Business management."

"Wow, impressive." I'm about to ask why she's back at the docks working when she has a degree under her belt, but fall silent when she speaks.

"I'm in the car with a registered nurse and two professional NHL players." She laughs. "That's impressive."

"You're impressive too, Charlie."

She frowns, and I'm not sure what it is I'm sensing, but my gut tells me she's a little lost, a little unhappy with the course of her life. Although I'm not sure that's it at all. I do wonder, however, why she left the city to go back home. Does she feel stuck helping out in the family business? Everyone knows she grew up without a father and her mother and sisters have been running the business. Yet her mother said she wanted her daughters to have experiences.

I resist the urge to slide my hand across the seat and squeeze hers. Not just because there is a sadness in her eyes, but because I want to touch her. That would be overstepping boundaries, and while she might not like men in a romantic way, she doesn't like me in *any* way, and I've yet to figure out why.

We reach our destination and I pull into a parking spot. We get out of the car, and I walk around the front and step up to Charlie. "I just remembered something."

"What?" Charlie asks.

"I hate shopping. How about you girls shop, and Rider and I hit up a patio for a beer."

"Nope," Jules says. "I want my man's opinion on what I buy, plus he needs things too."

I groan, and reluctantly follow them into the store. "I guess I could use a new pair of hikers."

We get inside the store, and we follow Charlie around. She points out what we'll need for the boat and hiking, and while she provides the tents, camping supplies, and food—I'm pretty sure I read that somewhere on the brochure, although I only glanced at it—she suggests we bring clothing for different weather conditions. We load up a cart and while Charlie is looking for the perfect raincoat for herself, trying a few on in front of a mirror, I pick up a pair of boots, and examine them.

Jules comes over, a little smile on her face, and I'm glad she's having a good time shopping.

"What do you think, Jules?" I ask and hold the boots up.

"I think you two make a cute couple."

My head jerks her way. "What?"

"Come on, Wes." She picks up a pair of boots, examines them and sets them back on the shelf. "Don't pretend you're not interested. I see the way you look at her."

My shoulders sag. "Oh, you saw that, did you?" No sense in hiding the truth from Jules. She's too smart for that. "But she's...you know, what Breton said."

She gives a low laugh and shakes her head. "Breton has no idea what she's talking about. She obviously wants you back, and probably said that out of spite."

"You think Charlie is into guys?" I ask, not that I really should be getting involved with her. I'm only here for a couple more weeks, and as for a little fun, she doesn't seem the type for a hook-up. I don't want her to look at me as a ticket out of here, either. Been there, done that, and have the scars to prove it. Which makes me wonder why I'm asking, "Do you think she likes... me?" God, I sound immature and pathetic.

Her grin widens. "She's really throwing you off, isn't she?"

"Meaning?"

"You're a smart guy, Wes. You can figure it out."

4

CHARLIE

After we pay for our purchases, we step back outside and the sun is lower on the horizon as tourists flock to the downtown core. The sweet smell of the ocean as well as delicious food smells from all the vendors lining the shore fill the air. We load our stuff into the trunk and because it's a gorgeous evening, I'd really love to hit the waterfront and grab something to eat before we go back home.

I turn to Jules as she stuffs numerous bags into the trunk. I laugh at all her purchases, and some things for little Sophie too. It was fun to hang out with her, and her husband, and... okay, it was fun to hang out with Wes, too. But seriously, I really enjoyed the shopping and girl talk with someone other than my three younger sisters.

"Do you want to grab a beaver tail?" I ask, and both Jules and Rider look at me with a mixture of curiosity and quiet concern in their eyes.

"Ah, what's a beaver tail?" Jules asks, her nose crinkled, and I open my mouth about to explain when Wes puts his hand on my shoulder to stop me. The heat from his skin seeps into me, and just like that—like a switch is being flicked from off to on—heat bombards every inch of my body. I hope and pray no one can tell what's going on inside me. The truth is, his touch is anything but sexual, and my nipples should not be reacting with enthusiasm.

"Let me," he says, his lips quirking, and I quickly catch on. "A beaver tail is a Canadian thing. Dessert. We eat them."

Jules fumbles back a step, her eyes are wide, and her mouth is opening and closing as she stares at us, a minute of shock and repulsion on her pretty face. As her lashes blink rapidly over dark eyes, Wes and I exchange a knowing glance, and I telegraph a secret message that I'm willing to play along, have a little fun with his friends.

"Yeah," I say, jumping in as he steps a bit closer, nudging me gently, happy that I'm game to mess with his friends. "We have them with maple, or coconut or chocolate." I briefly close my eyes and lick my lips. "Mmm...delicious."

Wes rubs his stomach, and my gaze follows the motion. What would those hard abs feel like beneath my fingers? God, I really need to stop thinking about him sexually. I'm beginning to lose my mind. "My favorite is hazelnut spread and bananas."

"The Banarama," I say and he gives me a wide grin, his eyes glistening with a smile. It's weird, because as I look at him, play along like we're thick as thieves, I can't help but feel this strange bond weaving between us. It's not smart to let these weird emotions tug at me, but I'm not sure there is anything I can do about it as we playfully conspire and share secrets.

"What do you like, Charlie?" Wes asks and it takes me a minute to register his words, but there's a heat in his eyes, and for the briefest of seconds I can't help but think he's asking what I like...sexually.

Get it together, girl.

"Mine is the classic, a beaver tail covered in sugar and cinnamon," I blurt out, hoping I sound normal, and not ridiculously aroused. "So good."

I struggle to keep the grin from my face, as Rider blinks, his lips twisted in derision as we moan over the pastry dessert.

"You eat a beaver's tail?" Rider asks, his voice loud, horrified, and he adjusts his ball cap, his eyes darting around, completely unsure of the situation. He backs up to where Jules is standing, and I keep the grin from my face.

Wes does the same with his cap, readjusting it over his mess of hair. "Oh yeah, so good. Come on. This is one Canadian experience you can't miss."

Jules holds her hands up. "I am not eating a beaver's tail, Wes. I'm willing to try new things but not that."

"We all know I'm a thrill seeker, but uh uh, no fucking way."

Wes laughs, working hard to keep it together, and I step closer, almost behind him to hide the laughter fighting its way out of my throat.

"But you'll love it," We assure them.

Jules holds both hands up, palms out. "The fact that you knit is strange, Wes, but now I find out you eat beaver's tails."

Rider shakes his head. "Canadians are fucking weird."

Wes and I burst out laughing, neither of us able to hold it in a second longer. I put my hand on his back, and his muscles quake beneath my fingers. "Americans, eh?" Wes says with a jerk of his head.

"Hosers," I add as we laugh harder, but our American friends look less than impressed. I pull myself together, step up to Jules and loop my arm through hers.

"Maybe we can head to Timmie's and get a double-double to go with our beaver tails?" Wes says. "You haven't lived until you tasted a double-double Timmie's." He shoves a hand into his shorts pocket, and roots around. "I think I have a couple of loonies and toonies in my pocket," he adds speaking faster as he throws around our Canadian slang. "Maybe we can even get a two-four on the way home."

"Who is Timmy, and what is a double-double?" Rider asks. "And can you slow down, I can hardly understand what you're saying."

Jules scrunches her nose. "And what's a two-four?"

"We'll show you," I say, enjoying our shared joke far too much, and I hate to admit it, but Wes is a lot of fun. Seriously though, letting Americans think we eat the beavers' tails never gets old.

"As long as I don't have to eat a beaver or anyone named Timmie," Jules says. "I'm all about experiencing Canada, but I draw the line at that. It's just—"

"Delicious," I blurt out.

She shakes her head at me. "No, Charlie. It's weird. Just weird."

Laughing, I tug Jules along and we cross the street. We pass by a few high-end shops and she stops to gaze at the fancy dresses. I think the last time I wore a dress was to my graduation. While I don't mind dressing up, since every now and then it's fun, I much prefer my comfy clothes.

Jules gasps and points to a dress. "That one would look amazing on you, Charlie."

I examine the sexy black cocktail dress and picture myself in it. "You think?"

"You have the perfect body for it."

"Maybe I could wear it."

She laughs. "Surely you must go out to a nice dinner every now and then."

"Every now and then," I say. "There are a couple of great restaurants here in the city that I can recommend if you and Rider decide to go."

"You'll come with us." It's a statement, not a question.

"I don't know about that," I say. "I don't want to be a third wheel."

"You wouldn't be. Wes is the third wheel." She winks at me playfully. "It'd be fun to go on a double date."

"I'm not going on a date with Wes."

"You don't think he's a good catch?" she asks.

"A good catch is four hundred full lobster traps a day," I tease, my gaze sliding to Wes, to his perfect ass in his khakis, to be precise.

She laughs and wanting a change of topic, I drag her along to the boardwalk where all the small vendors are set up. I wave my hand at the big red building sporting the sign, Beaver Tails.

"The best artisanal pastry around." I point to the Tim Horton's kiosk. "That's Timmie's, best coffee around, and a double-double is double cream, double sugar. It's the only way to get your coffee."

Jules folds her arms. "I can't believe you let me believe you ate beavers' tails! I thought Canadians were nice."

I laugh. "We *are* nice. I promise."

She gives me a doubtful glare and Wes laughs. "Don't blame her. She was just playing along, and for the record, a hoser is a polite term used by Canadians to say someone is clueless." Wes claps his hand on his buddy's shoulder. "We were just messing with you guys, and a two-four is a twenty-four pack of beer, which I'll buy, since you two are such good sports."

Rider just shakes his head and I nudge Wes, but the second I do, need zings through me. I swallow, but the truth is I love this comradery between us. "What is this I hear about you knitting, huh?"

He puts his finger to his lips. "Shh, that's a secret, but if you want, I can hook you up with a toque. I might have an extra one or two laying around."

Picturing this muscular guy sitting by a winter's fire with knitting needles in his hands brings a laugh to my lips. It also warms me in the oddest ways, because it's actually kind of sexy...and freaking adorable.

I blink up at him, curious, wanting to know more about his life. "Who taught you?"

"Are we still talking about this?" he asks.

"If you don't tell me, I'm going to shout it out loud. Let the entire world know that tough NHL player Wes Hatfield knits."

He tugs my hair playfully. "Fine then, but I must warn you. If you do, I might have to kiss you again just to shut you up."

God, I wish I didn't like the idea of that so much.

"You two are like an old married couple." Rider laughs.

I roll my eyes at Rider, but now I'm suddenly wondering why Wes isn't attached, engaged, or married like his best bud. I think Jules is right. He is a catch. But I'm guessing he's probably having too much fun with all the puck bunnies who throw themselves at him. Not that I care. I don't. He can sleep with anyone he wants. And now I'm mad at myself because my stupid mind is visualizing what it would be like to have him in my bed, those big hands all over my body.

"His grandmother taught his mother and they both taught him," Jules explained. "I was curious about the whole knitting thing too, so I asked last night."

"There you go, Charlie. You can thank Jules. She just saved you from having to kiss me again."

I think I might be mad at Jules. "Thank you, Jules," I say, and twist my lips. "You know, in Newfoundland, it's tradition to kiss a cod."

"Eww, did you do that?"

"Well…" I say, teasing as I glance at Wes.

A chuckle rumbles in his throat, and wraps around me in the most erotic ways. "It was a rushed kiss. Not my best work. If you'd like me to—"

Oh, yes please.

"Nope I'm good."

Laughing, Wes pulls his wallet from his pocket and grins at me. "I'm buying, what do you all want?"

"I can get my own," I tell him.

"And I can buy."

"But—"

"What was that you said about not being stubborn?"

I lift my chin an inch. Dammit, he got me there. "Nothing."

"Fine, I'm buying. A thank you for coming with us. Jules really enjoyed your company."

I'm about to ask if he did too when I catch myself. I don't really care if he enjoyed my company or not. The truth is I *shouldn't* care if he enjoyed my company. He was so mean to me years ago, and I don't want to let myself get close to a guy who's only here for a few summer weeks. Been there, done that. I take in his profile as he walks up to the counter, and a powerful kind of want grips me. Rider joins him, and they place their order. Jules loops her arm around mine and I take in her grin.

"He might not be your catch of the day, but you can't deny he's cute," she says.

"What?"

"Wes, he's a real cutie."

I shrug. "I guess. I haven't really noticed." A sudden shriek pierces my ear. "What the—"

"Here we go," Jules says, and I frown, not understanding. I turn to see a group of girls running up to the guys, and they both adjust their hats again. That's when I realize why they wear them pulled low. But two handsome men, NHL players or not, are bound to grab attention everywhere they go, no matter how hard they try to keep a low profile. As I study Wes' body language, it's pretty clear that he doesn't enjoy the limelight. I guess he grew up working alone on the farm and prefers his privacy.

"Wow, does this happen all the time?" I ask Jules.

"All the time." Both Wes and Rider smile and are very gracious and accommodating as the girls ask for autographs and take selfies.

I stand back and watch, an uneasy feeling in the pit of my stomach. I swallow, and I think back to my last boyfriend. He was good looking. Not as good looking as Wes, but he was charming and outgoing, and women loved him, much like they love these two guys. He worked the docks with his uncle for one summer, and applied for jobs out west. Honestly, I never should have gotten emotionally involved with a guy who was only visiting. When the season ended, he landed his dream job and wanted me to go with him. Alberta didn't have the ocean, and it meant changing everything for him, and I wouldn't be happy doing that. In the end, I didn't go. I can't be what someone else wants me to be, and he had no trouble replacing me with another local. Last I heard, they had three kids.

Is it possible that I'd change things up, make compromises, if it was with...a different guy? Or would fear of heartbreak and loss keep me grounded?

That thought catches me off guard, and sets my brain buzzing as my gaze goes to Rider, as he bends to let a girl kiss his cheek during a selfie. My heart stalls, and worry for my friend clutches my heart. "Do you..." I catch myself before I finish. This is not my business.

"Do I ever get jealous, worried?" she asks.

"Sorry, I should never have gone there. It's not my business." Plus, I don't want to plant ideas in her head.

"I love Rider. He loves me. We also trust each other." Rider's head lifts, a little check-in on his wife. He gives her a wink, a secret message between them and she smiles at him.

"That's really sweet."

"Yeah," she says dreamily. She takes a deep breath. "I'm a lucky girl."

"He's a lucky guy too."

"Thank you. You're sweet, and honestly, Charlie, what they're doing there, that isn't who they are. Not deep inside. They're putting on a show for fans, giving them what they want. Outside of that, they're real men with values and integrity. It's all about looking deeper and separating the player from the man."

As her words bounce around inside my brain, my gaze goes to Wes as he plays it up for the selfies. "Does Wes...I mean, um, is he, has he ever been serious with anyone?"

"Nope." She bumps me with her hip. "And despite what you think, he's a real catch."

I laugh. "I'm not looking for a relationship, especially not with a guy like him."

"What does that mean?"

"Just that he's a local celebrity, and the papers watch him carefully. Lots of pictures of him with girls all over him."

"Don't believe everything you hear." She points to the guys. "Or half of what you see."

I nod. What was it Breton said about me the other day: I played for the other team? I guess I'm judged by what I wear and what I do all the time. No one has ever really taken the time to get to know the girl beneath the coveralls, figure out who I really am, or what I really want. Is it the same for Wes?

When our pastry order is up, both Wes and Rider excuse themselves and the girls all walk away, giggling and laughing. Wes walks up to me and hands over the beaver tail, acting like he hadn't just been accosted by a group of girls. I thank him and take a bite of the warm pastry.

I moan, and briefly close my eyes as the flavor explodes on my tongue. "Ohmigod, this is so good." I open my eyes and find Wes staring at me, his jaw clenched tight, those caramel eyes a shade darker. "What?" I ask and brush the cinnamon sugar from my face. His chest rises and falls as he swallows, hard.

"I'll have what she's having," Jules says with a laugh, and that's when I realize what's going on. I might as well have been making love to the damn pastry. A little embarrassed, I turn from Wes, hoping he can't see the heat traveling into my cheeks, and I probably shouldn't examine the way he was watching me, with heat...lust...want.

Although I could be mistaken. I'm not like any of the girls he's been with. Breton is a fine example. Head cheerleader, gorgeous, most popular girl back in high school. Not my business, I guess. Still, I can't help but wonder why he wanted to kiss me in front of her, pretend we're a couple. Can't help but want him to kiss me again.

Ohmigod, girl, get over yourself.

"Charlie," Jules yells. "This is the best thing I've ever eaten."

I grin, and turn to her, working to pull myself together. "Told you."

"I'm going to move to Canada and eat beaver tails all day," she says, and we laugh.

I shade the late day sun from my eyes and glance down the bustling boardwalk. "Come on, let's walk."

For the next hour, we stroll the gorgeous waterfront and stop to admire the boats in the water, as well as the sailboats catching the harbor breeze. The sweet smells of cotton candy and sugar cones fill the air as tourists on bicycles and scooters zip by us.

"Look," I say and point to the harbor hopper, an amphibious tour vehicle that goes from the water to the land.

"I want to do that." Jules says.

"Next time," Wes says. "We should be heading back. We all have a busy day tomorrow."

"Right," I agree doing a mental checklist of all the things I need to do before I take this group out on a weekend tour. It's odd that I'm a little excited to be spending more time with them. This side hustle was just to put the boat to use when we were between lobster seasons, and summer business for my sisters for when I finally move away and put my degree to use.

We make our way back to the car and I'm tired yet content as I slide in next to Wes. We chat quietly on the drive home, and since Wes' house is before mine, he drops off his friends.

"I can walk the rest of the way," I tell him and reach for the handle.

His hand juts out, and he captures my wrist. I spin to face him, and that grin on his face—my God, could he be any cuter—sends heat charging through me.

"I'm driving."

"I actually have to go to my boat. There are some things I need to do before morning."

"To the boat it is," he says and doesn't let go of my hand right away. Nope, his fingers linger on my arm, and zaps of electricity charge through me. I take a fast breath, and look at his hand on me and he withdrawals it.

I sink back into my seat, and he pulls back onto the road. We both remain quiet, lost in thought as he drives me to the dock. He parks near my boat and I practically jump from the car, needing to put a measure of distance between us. He climbs out too, goes to the trunk to get my shopping bags and takes two cans of beer from the two-four he bought.

He steps up to me, and taking me by surprise he casually throws his arm around my shoulder, like it's something we do all the time. I eye him, but he's not looking at me. I'm about to ask why his arm is around me, when he pulls me close, but that's when I see Breton walking our way, still in her work uniform. Oh, I get it.

I can't say as I hate the way his body is pressed to mine. I mean, I wish I did, but well, he's big and strong and so warm, and I of course can't forget this is all for show.

He sets my bags down, drops to the dock, his legs dangling over the end, and pats the deck beside him. I sit beside him, and he cracks a beer and hands it to me. I take a much-needed sip, willing my racing heart to slow as I glance at the gorgeous pink and purple streaks bruising the sky as the sun sets in the distance. It never gets old.

"Sorry about that," he says.

I shrug. "No worries, I get it."

"At least I didn't spring a kiss on you again."

"At least," I say.

"That would have been horrible, huh?"

"The worst."

He grins and takes a big drink of beer as I go back to admiring the sunset. I take a rejuvenating breath. "So beautiful."

"Yeah, beautiful," he agrees, but when I turn to him, he's looking at me not the sky. My pulse jumps in my throat, but I quickly remind myself Breton is nearby and he's just pretending to like me.

Right?

$$5$$

WES

"Ready to see some whales?" Charlie asks, a big smile on her pretty face as she adjusts her pink ball cap over her mess of windblown curls. My gaze falls over her, and I take in her rubber boots, her pantlegs tucked into them, and the loose knit sweater she's wearing over a T-shirt. It's something I could have knitted, and while it's big on her, it's sexy as hell.

"Do you really think we'll see them?" Jules asks, her eyes wide with excitement as her big new boots clunk on the wharf.

"I can't guarantee it, but we have a pretty good shot." I step onto the boat, and Rider follows. He turns to hold his hand out to Jules and she follows us on. The boat isn't big, the space is small and intimate, but I don't mind at all.

"Do you think you packed enough?" Charlie asks Jules with a laugh, when Rider drops an overstuffed duffle bag to the deck, and Jules shrugs out of her backpack. I glance around for tenting supplies, but only see one bag, and a backpack inside the cabin.

"I wanted to make sure I was prepared for rain, sun or snow," Jules explains.

I laugh. "I think Charlie said rain or shine. There's no snow this time of year." I glance at Charlie and roll my eyes. "Americans, they all think we live in igloos and eat whale blubber."

"I do not," Jules says and whacks me. "Besides, you live in Seattle. You're one of us, now." She crinkles her nose. "Well, you still knit, so maybe you're not."

"You can take the boy out of Canada, but you can't take the Canada out of the boy, eh?" Charlie says and laughs as she unties the boat from the dock, and wraps the rope around that metal thing anchored to the deck. I think she called it a cleat or something.

Jules pauses, and puts her arm on Rider. "Did you pack the bug spray?"

He laughs and kisses her forehead, and I grin. I'm not sure I've ever seen her so excited and while I'm happy for them I can't deny that deep inside I might be a bit envious of what they have.

"Yes, I've got everything," he says. "And we're only a boat ride away if we forgot something and have to return."

"I've got lots of bug spray, and suntan lotion, and everything else you might need," Charlie says, although I can't for the life of me figure out where she's storing it. She only has those two bags with her. "Have a seat." She points to the wooden benches on either side of the boat. "I'll get us out of here. Before I do, is there anyone you need to call, because once we're out there and on Brier Island, you can forget all about reliable cell reception."

"We called home already, and Sophie is having a blast with her aunt," Jules says.

Charlie turns to me. "How about you, Wes? Anyone going to lose their mind if they don't hear from you for a couple days?"

"Is this your way of trying to find out if I'm single?"

She rolls her eyes at me. "Oh please..."

"The answer is no, and yes. No one will miss me, and yes, I'm single."

"I'm sure the whales will be happy to hear that, and they'll likely find you far more charming than I do." She gives me a sassy wink and spins. Rider laughs, and claps me on the back.

"You've got your work cut out for you, bud."

I grin. I kind of like the chase, even though I shouldn't be chasing her. "Isn't that half the fun? And trust me, I know Jules gave you a run for your money."

"That I did," Jules says, and drops onto the bench seat as Charlie disappears inside the cabin to get us moving. Instead of sitting, I walk to the entrance of the cabin.

"Impressive," I say, and Charlie glances at me over her shoulder.

"If you don't sit and follow the rules while I'm piloting this boat, I'll make you wear a life jacket."

"Can I sit in here?" I ask, as I glance at the bench.

"Fine, as long as you don't distract me. I need to get out to open water without running into any other vessels."

She certainly doesn't look like she's having any trouble maneuvering away from the dock, but I sit, and the thing is, I kind of want to distract her. I like her attention. Juvenile, I know. "You're pretty good at piloting this thing."

"Been doing it for as long as I can remember."

She increases the thrust and slowly turns the wheel. "You really are impressive." She casts me a suspicious glance. "What?" I say with a laugh. "It's a compliment. I don't know many, or any, women who can do what you do."

She goes quiet for a second, and I can't help but think I've insulted her somehow. "Do you..." She gestures to the big wheel. "Want to try?"

Really? She's going to trust me with her boat. "I would love to."

"Let me just get us a little further out."

I stare at her, take in the jut of her hip, unable to take my eyes off her as she effortlessly steers us into deeper water. It would be nice to see a whale. Jules really wants to, but I'd be happy to spend the day watching Charlie handle this craft like it's an extension of herself.

"Who taught you how to pilot this thing?" I ask.

She smiles and I sense I've hit on a happier subject. "My grandfather did. He grew up on the boats. Like my mom, the sea was in his soul."

"It's in yours, too, isn't it?"

Her smile falls fast and I swear she's giving me whiplash. But what did I say to upset her?

"I had a couple of job interviews in Toronto," she blurts out and then groans like she's wondering why she's sharing that with me.

"Oh yeah."

She rubs her hand along the steering wheel, a loving gentle touch, and my cock twitches, aching to be caressed just like that—by her. "My sister will take over the tours."

"Sounds like you'll miss it."

She shrugs. "I have a degree to put to use, Wes. I interviewed with some great firms."

I take in the tightness of her body as I say, "You already put it to use, Charlie. I'm guessing you started these tours."

"It's a side gig. Puts the boat to use when we're not hauling lobsters, and keeps the business running." She glances at me. "Come here."

I climb from the bench and stand beside her. "Get behind me," she says, and goddammit, blood drains to my cock as I visualize her saying those words under different circumstances. I marshal my cock into submission, and stand behind her. "Put your hands right here."

I reach around her small body, and place my hands on the wheel. I inch a little closer to get a better grip and my body presses against hers, and I swallow, praying to fuck my dick doesn't jump to attention, and poke her in the back.

Her voice is low, almost mesmerized when she asks, "How does that feel?"

Jesus.

"Nice," I say.

She takes one of my hands and puts it on the throttle. "Now, when you increase the thrust, you can feel her power." She puts her hand over mine, and slowly pushes it forward. The boat speeds up. "Fun, huh?" she asks, a slight quiver in her voice. Is she feeling this pull between us every bit as much as I am?

"It is fun."

"Not as fun as hockey though, right?"

I laugh. "Different."

She goes quiet for a minute, and I continue to steer the boat, my arms around her. She finally breaks the silence and asks, "Do you like what you do, Wes?"

"I love the game, yeah."

She casts a glance at me over her shoulder. "But?"

I laugh. "You sensed a but in there, did you?" She nods, and I'm not about to tell her that deep in my soul I can't help but feel something is missing. "No buts. I love it."

"It's great you get to do what you love."

There's a longing in her voice. What is she thinking? What is it she's longing for? If I had to guess I'd say it was to get out of rural Nova Scotia, like every other person our age, but to see her on this boat, I'd say it's where she belonged. There's no doubt I belong in a rink and while I do love it, there are times it's a bit lonely too. Most of the guys are finding their partners now. I'm the rookie, still learning his way around, and while there's a bunny always ready to warm my bed, that gets old too. I guess what's missing from my soul is a family of my own.

"I'm glad you made it, Wes."

That deep yearning in her voice wraps around my heart. "You'll make it too, Charlie. I'm sure both of those firms in Toronto will make an offer and you'll have your pick."

She nods. "You're probably right. You know, I loved playing hockey like you did, but I definitely didn't want to make a career out of it," she says with a sigh. "Mom wanted us to try everything. I think she'll be disappointed if I don't get a job in the city."

Odd, I never really sensed that about her mom, and Charlie *wants* to leave, right? To me it just seemed like her mom wanted her daughters to try everything, to discover who they are, and have no regrets. As I think about her mother's wisdom, I want to ask about her dad. All I ever knew was that he left when she was just a kid. What kind of guy walks out on his wife and four young daughters? While I'd like to know, I don't want to bring up another subject that might upset her.

"You were damn good at hockey." As I think back to her aggressiveness on the ice, an idea hits. "Hey, maybe we can have a game of one-on-one before I leave."

As soon as the words fall off my tongue, I realize how sexual they sounded. She doesn't call me on it. Instead, she taps my hand and I remove it from the throttle to put it back on the wheel. "You're a natural, Wes. I'm not surprised."

"Why not?" I ask, and lower my head until my mouth is close to her ear. Her sweet floral scent curls around me and there isn't a goddamn thing I can do to stop my dick from swelling.

"You're the kind of guy who's good at everything he does. A natural athlete, farmer, and now fisherman."

"Thanks for the compliment but I'll leave the fishing stuff to you." Needing a reprieve from her body, I let go of the wheel and step back. It's either that, or I'm going to put my mouth on her neck, and my hands...everywhere.

I'm a little breathless and lightheaded as I drop back onto the bench. Honestly, the last time I wanted a woman this badly was...never.

"Are you okay?" her eyes narrow in on me. "Oh no."

"What?" I ask.

"I think you might be getting seasick. Sometimes that can happen when you first take over the wheel."

"Yeah," I agree. It's better to let her think I'm woozy from steering the boat. She'd probably throw me overboard if she knew it was from standing so close and touching her sweet body.

"Open my bag." She gestures with a nod. "I have something for that."

"I'm okay. Besides, I don't want to get sleepy. I want to be wide awake for this."

She eyes me for a moment longer. "Go on out back, and get some air. I'll be slowing us down soon."

I'd like to stay and watch her, but I step out from the cabin and find Rider and Jules looking over the side of the boat as waves splash up and Jules laughs in delight.

"Find anything interesting down there?"

Jules turns and gives me a knowing look, and points to the cabin. "I could ask the same about you."

"I was learning to steer this vessel," I say and she just grins. I get it. She'd like to see us hook up. Hell, I would too. But Charlie doesn't really like me, and she doesn't strike me as the kind of girl to engage in a summer fling—especially with a guy who has a reputation and will be hitting the road soon. She too will be moving to the big city of Toronto.

The boat slows, and Charlie shouts to us from the cabin. "Over there, guys."

We all turn and look out the other side and Jules squeals when she sees a great big whale off in the distance. It jumps from the water and lands with a huge splash. I glance at the cabin and find Charlie watching us, a huge smile on her face. We all grab our phones and start taking pictures, as Charlie slowly inches the boat closer, no doubt being careful to give the big mammals a wide berth. Once she gets us close, a couple of hundred meters away, she kills the engine, and steps out of the cabin.

"Beautiful, aren't they?"

"Yeah," I say and take in her big smile as the wind blows her hat off her head. I try to snatch it, before it gets carried away, but I'm too late.

"I should have known better," she says.

"Sorry, I thought I had it."

"My own fault. I know better than to wear a ball cap, that the wind can take. You'd think lessons learned."

"Not the first hat you've lost, I take it."

"I think I'm a slow learner," she says with a laugh.

"Good thing I brought this for you then." I unzip my bag and pull out a gray knitted hat and her eyes go wide.

"You brought this for me."

"Yeah," I say feeling oddly foolish. Was that a strange thing to do?

"This is so nice." She runs her hand over the wool and tugs it on and my heart squeezes a little tighter in my chest. "I love it, Wes."

"Looks great on you."

She tucks her hair into it, and laughs. "Did you make this?" I nod, and the happiness in her voice curls around me, arousing me... A pink blush spreads across her cheeks as she stares at the whale playing, and I have no doubt that she's in her element out here and honestly with the wind blowing tendrils of hair around her face, she's never looked more adorable.

The boat rocks and we all bump around. I smack into Charlie, and she puts her hand on my arm to keep me from falling. "Told you. No sea legs." She makes a tsking sound, and I tug on her long curls playfully and she whacks my chest. I close my hand over hers and keep it on my body, wanting her to touch me. She blinks up at me, and I don't miss the tightening of her lips, the way my heart beats just a little faster when she's close. I bet she can feel it beneath her fingers.

"You're kind of a smart ass," I say. A smart ass I want to take to my bed in the worst fucking way. I keep that to myself, though. For now. Maybe later, when we're on land, and she can't throw me overboard, I'll let her know what being around her does to me, and give her a kiss she'll never forget. One thing is for certain, I know better than to get in deep with a girl who wants bigger and better, because when it comes right down to it, I'm a simple farm boy at heart, who just happens to be good at hockey. I've learned girls aren't interested in that guy, and I'm not going to make that mistake again.

Then again, maybe like Charlie, I'm a slow learner…

I grab my phone from my back pocket and take a few pictures. "This never gets old," I say, hoping my voice doesn't come out sounding breathless and aroused, because yeah, that's what touching Wes does to me. Who am I kidding? Just standing next to him on my boat, makes my knees weak and here I was teasing *him* about having no sea legs when I'm about to go down for the count.

Honestly though, I can still feel the burning imprint of his muscles as they tightened and clenched beneath my fingers, his strong heartbeat as it thudded against my palm. When we get to Brier Island, the first thing I'm going to do is take a dip into the cold ocean. Either that, or I'm going to throw myself at him and beg him to take me.

I get that I'm not his type and that I don't fit into his world. I'm not a put together, sexy bunny or any sort of socialite. I'm the opposite of all those things. Still though, there are times, like when I touch him that none of that seems to matter—that this man wants me. The truth is, I have been a bit lonely.

My friends are all gone, and I have my family and my work, but some things…I don't know, I crave more.

But getting involved with Wes isn't a smart idea. It can't go anywhere. We live in different worlds. Then again, does it have to go anywhere? Can't I for once in my life, just have a casual hook-up? It's not my style, but there's nothing wrong with it either.

I let my gaze fall over him as I consider that. I take in his smile as he snaps pictures, and there's no denying I want him, that my body is screaming at me to climb him like a goddamn tree. Maybe I should. Maybe I should climb into his tent tonight and seduce him. One night. One hook-up. Tomorrow, things go back to normal. It's been so long since a man put his hands on my body, I forget what it's like to be touched. If I go into this knowing it's a one-time thing, what could it hurt? It's not like I'm going to fall for him. He's a player and I'm smarter than that and it's not like he's going to ask me to leave with him, and when I say no, quickly replace me with someone who will.

"You okay?" Wes asks.

"Yeah, why?"

He angles his head. "You looked like you were a million miles away there."

"Just ah…thinking about my uh, equipment," I fib. Good Lord, I'm not going to come right out and tell him I was thinking about his equipment. "Doing a mental check of the things we need to set up tonight."

Just then another whale pops out of the water and I'm grateful for the distraction. "Omigod, look, two of them now."

Jules claps her hands and everyone starts snapping pictures again. One of the whales comes closer to the boat, curious about us, and it breaches and lands with a big splash, soaking us from head to toe. We turn from the spray, laughing and sputtering and checking to make sure our phones aren't ruined.

I wipe water from my face and take in Wes' wet T-shirt as it clings to his skin. With my wool sweater soaked, I peel it off, and remove my hat, but I'm drenched all the way through to my T-shirt.

The whale comes up again and gives us all another splash and the boat rocks. We're all laughing and banging into one another and the next thing I know, Wes' arms are around me, my body crushed against his as we sway together. My nipples take that moment to harden, and no it's not from the cold splash of water.

"I think he's messing with us," Wes says, his voice an octave lower.

"You know they say if you get showered by a whale, it's supposed to bring good luck."

"Really?"

I shrug. "It's an old wives' tale." It's been a long time since I've seen the whales perform for people, and I have to say, it's a lot of fun watching them. Jeez, when was the last time I had this much fun on the water with customers? Then again, none of them were homeboy Wes Hatfield. He is kind of fun...and nice to hang out with.

"So you're saying I'm going to get lucky?" Wes teases.

"Maybe with her. She's the one who finds you charming," I clarify and point toward the water.

He angles his head, that sexy grin of his doing ridiculous things to my body. "You think she likes me?"

Who doesn't?

"I don't know about that, but what I do know is that I'm all wet," I say, stating the obvious, but then heat jumps into my cheeks when I meet his gaze and realize what I just said, and how it could be taken as sexual. "I mean..."

"Yeah, we're all wet," Wes says and let's go of me. "It's a good thing we all brought a lot of extra clothes." He reaches over his back, and peels his shirt off with ease, and I swear to God, my legs go so wobbly, I nearly topple overboard. I sink down onto a bench seat as he fishes a dry shirt out of his bag, and shakes it out.

Rider and Jules root for clean clothes too, and I should probably get the boat into motion so we don't drift out to sea, but I'd have to stop staring and drooling, and I'm not in much of a hurry to do that.

He tugs on his shirt, and I wish erotic dance music wasn't playing in my head, but alas it is, and there isn't a damn thing I can do about it.

"Did you bring a dry shirt, or do you want to borrow one of mine?" Jules asks, as she dries her face with a towel.

"I uh...think..."

"Here," Wes says and tosses me one of his. "It's big, but it should do the trick."

"Oh, okay, thanks." Even though I have my own clothes, I take the shirt and bring it to my nose to breathe in the fresh scent of fabric softener. I stand. "I'll just dart into the cabin and change."

"I'm coming with you," Jules says. "I'm not much into flashing whales, or Wes."

"Too late for me, Jules."

My jaw drops. "You flashed Wes."

She laughs, and covers her face. "There was this bathing suit incident one time when we were at Watauga Beach." She licks her finger and checks the air. "Bathing suit one, Jules zero."

We both laugh and head to the cabin, and I'm grateful I packed my one piece. Not that I think I'll be swimming, even though I'm completely overheated thanks to Wes. But the ocean is freaking cold. I tug off my T-shirt, and pull on Wes' shirt, tying it at the waist.

"Wes looks good on you," Jules says with a grin.

"You mean, Wes' shirt looks good on me."

"Maybe I don't." She glances out as the two men stand there and talk. "You really don't think he's cute?"

"No," I say and mean it. Wes isn't cute. He's drop dead gorgeous and I can't take my eyes off him.

She laughs at that. "Yeah, that's what I thought."

"We sort of have a history," I admit. "He wasn't always nice to me."

She frowns, and her head jerks back in shock. "Are you serious? Wes wasn't nice to you? He's nice to everyone. He's Canadian and that's like Canadian law or something, isn't it?"

I chuckle. "He said some things that weren't so nice."

She shakes her head. "Are you sure you're not mistaken? That doesn't sound like him. Even if it was, he's not that boy anymore, and you two make a cute couple."

"I'm not looking to be a couple, Jules."

She holds her hands up. "I'm sorry. Not my business, but it's the nurse in me, always prying, asking questions and making observations."

"It's okay. You don't have anything to be sorry about."

"Oh, okay then." She points to Wes who is staring right at us and jumps right back in with both feet, adding, "Then you might want to get yourself some of that, or you might be the one who's sorry."

My pulse leaps at her playfulness and I pray to God Wes can't hear her. "I like you, Jules. Don't make me throw you overboard."

She laughs at that and I turn my attention to the wheel as she steps from the cabin. I shake my head. I like her. A lot, and there is a part of me that thinks she's right. I start thinking about a hook-up again as I change course and head toward Brier Island. The sound of boots on the deck behind me, signals I'm not alone. I don't need to turn to know it's Wes. His energy surrounds me, and raises the hair on my skin in delightful ways that take my brain down a dirty path with a dirty farm boy who is good with his hands. I really should get behind that, or at least underneath it.

"Hey," he says and steps up behind me, close enough that I can smell his skin.

"Hey yourself."

"Everything okay?"

"Yeah. Just adjusting course."

"What uh, what did Jules say to you?" I glance over my shoulder to find him rubbing his chin.

"She just said your shirt looked good on me." And that I should jump your bones, but I think it's best if I leave that out.

"She can be a bit blunt at times. I think it's the nurse in her."

I point and redirect the conversation. If I keep thinking about his body, I'm liable to crash my boat. "See that right there?"

He leans over me, his breath hot on my face as he rests his chin on my shoulder. "Is that Brier Island?"

"Can you see the seals sunning themselves?"

"Wow, that's incredible."

"Call the others up here so they can see." He calls out to Jules and Rider and they squeeze into the cabin with us. "That's called seal cove," I tell them.

"There must be about forty seals there," Jules says, but I'm having a hard time concentrating on her words when Wes puts his hands on my hips for no good reason at all, other than to send heat flaring through me.

Jules points. "Look at that gorgeous lighthouse."

"It has a little café in it. They have the best cinnamon rolls."

"Wait, is that a hotel?" Rider asks.

I glance to the strip hotel with rooms overlooking the ocean. "Yeah, why?"

He looks aghast. "We're camping when the island has a hotel?"

"Oh, you hockey players and your luxury." I roll my eyes at Jules, but she too is looking at the hotel with longing. "We're roughing it for the next few nights, and really it's hardly roughing it."

"Why do you say that?" Wes asks.

"You read the brochure, didn't you?" I ask Wes.

"If by reading it, you mean that I glanced at it, then yes."

I laugh. "Ah, then you are all in for a real treat."

They all eye each other, but I keep my little secret. I point out landmarks as I steer us into the dock. I park at my usual spot and jump from the boat, to tie the rope to a cleat.

"Grab your bags," I say, and I'm about to hop back on and grab mine when Wes snatches them up and throws them over his shoulder.

"I can carry those." He angles his head and I just shrug, giving up before I get started. "Fine, you can carry them, too."

Jules stands on the rocking dock and lifts her face to the sun. "I might never leave here."

"Come on," I say and walk down the dock. Wes catches up to me, and his knuckles brush mine as we follow the path to the lighthouse, where my Jeep is stored. Good family friends, George and Roxane own the lighthouse café, and live on the island, so they let me keep my vehicle here, which makes life so much easier for me. They also manage my business from here and restock the tents and fridges for me.

"This is so quaint," Jules says as we walk up the stone steps toward the lighthouse. I stop by my Jeep. "How are you at hotwiring?" I ask Wes and his head goes back, his eyes wide, and alarmed, forcing me to bite back a grin.

"You're kidding, right?"

"Of course, I'm kidding. I don't need any man hotwiring anything for me. I can do it all by myself." I wink at him and head inside the lighthouse. They all follow me in.

"Good morning, Roxane."

Her head lifts and she jumps up when she sees its me, lifting a portion of the counter and throwing her arms out. It was just last week I was out here getting things set up for the summer season but with her, it's like it's been decades.

Before her arms reach me, her face falls and she goes still, her gaze going to a spot behind me, to Wes and Rider obviously.

"What the..." She gives me an evil eye. "You didn't tell me you were hosting Wes Hatfield and Rider Lewis." She wags a finger at me. "You sneak."

I laugh and she hugs me. "I wanted to surprise you." I glance at the guys and crinkle my nose in apology to Wes. He's always a good sport, but it's clear he doesn't like to be the center of attention. "She's a big fan."

"Scooch out of the way," she says to me, and Jules and Rider exchange a playful look, no doubt laughing at our Canadian slang. She hugs each man, and then turns to pull Jules in for a hug. Yeah, some Canadians are huggers.

Once finished, she hands me a set of keys, and frowns. "What?" I ask, taking in the worried look on her face.

"I'm afraid there was a bit of trouble at your place last night."

"Trouble?"

"Animals," she says.

"Oh no."

"George is out there now, trying to fix it, but it will take a bit before we can get a new mattress. Something nested in it, but you have the two other tents for your guests, and you can always stay with us, you know that?"

I nod. Her offer is a nice one, but I don't like to intrude or be too far from my guests. This whole experience is about catering to them, and showing them around the island. Repeat business and reviews are important.

"I'll head out and check it out," I say. I find Wes frowning at me when I turn.

"Something got into your mattress?" he asks, completely confused and why wouldn't he be? He thinks we're sleeping on the ground in a tent, but this is so much better than that.

I click the fob on the Jeep, and we toss our stuff in the back. I glance at Wes. "Sorry for all her fussing. You're always so nice about it, though."

"I'd be nothing without my fans, so I don't mind." He shrugs. "I don't love being the center of attention in a big crowd or anything but one-on-one is okay. Speaking of one-on-one, are you still up for playing?"

I grin, not sure he's talking about hockey, as I pull onto the road, and a few minutes later I take the gravel path to the shore, where I worked really hard putting together a glamping site.

"Ohmigod," Jules squeals as the three dome tents come into view. "We're glamping."

"What the hell is glamping?" Wes asks.

I grin at him. "Glamorous camping." I stop the vehicle and wave. "Your dome awaits you."

Jules shrieks. "We really are in igloos."

I laugh. "Sort of."

I turn to Wes. "You might want to close your mouth. You don't want to catch a fly, not when I have a steak dinner planned for tonight."

"You...you did all this?"

"I might work the boats and the retail store, but I know things."

The shock and admiration on his face make me laugh when he says, "Yeah, you do."

"Do you like it?"

"What's not to like, Charlie? This is fantastic."

I point to Wes. "You're in dome one, and you two are in number two. Go check them out. Take your time, relax. There's food in the fridges. Eat, or have a nap if you want. This is all about relaxing and unwinding. I have a picnic planned, but nothing is in stone, and this is all about what you guys want to do." Wes shakes his head as he exits the vehicle, and as they run off to inspect their domes, I go find George in dome number three—my personal space.

I poke my head in. "Hey there," I say, a knot in my stomach when I take in the mess of foam some animal ripped from the mattress to make a cozy nest. I step inside when George turns to me. "How did it get in?"

"A tear in the canvas." He points upward. "I patched it up. It'll keep the elements out, but I'm afraid you won't have a bed to sleep on."

"Thanks so much George. I really appreciate it."

He grins. "That's what you pay me for."

"How long until we can get a mattress?" I ask.

George shakes his head. "About a week, until then you can sleep—"

"With me."

Charlie turns so fast, she almost trips over her boots, loses her balance and face plants. What, was it something I said?

"No, no nooooo," she says quickly, her long curls bouncing as she shakes her head. "You're here on a paid vacation, and I'm not going to crash in your dome and ruin it for you."

"Wouldn't be ruining it at all." I step inside and look at the mess left by animals. "Hey, we're old friends, neighbors really, and Canadian at that. I'm just being nice."

She opens and closes her mouth, like she's trying to find her words, find the right way to protest, but really, my dome has a big bed, and a bunk above it where you can unzip the dome and stare at the stars as you fall asleep. She thought of everything.

"You can take the bed or the bunk. I'm okay with either."

"I...um..."

"That's mighty nice of you, young man, and it makes perfect sense to me." George's blue eyes narrow in on me, and then his head jerks back like I might have just slapped him. "Jesus wept, and Moses slept, and Adam came on crutches."

I laugh, having heard my grandmother use those words when something surprised or shocked her.

"You're Wes Hatfield."

"I am," I say and hold my hand out for a shake. He readily accepts and gives my hand a good squeeze. "Nice to meet you, George." I catch the grin on Charlie's face. I think she's getting used to all the attention I get wherever I go.

"I'll be damned." He lets out a loud laugh. "The missus must have lost her mind when she saw you, and then talked your ear off."

I laugh with him. "She was quite gracious," I tell him.

He turns to Charlie. "Luv, I think staying in Wes' dome here is a great idea. No sense in letting the spare bed go unused or driving back to our place after dark. Traffic, you know."

She shakes her head, like the world is conspiring against her. "Yeah, a regular freeway here on the island where the ferry brings over all of ten cars at a time."

"Like I said, traffic."

Her gaze slides to mine and her freckles bunch as she crinkles her nose. "You sure I won't be imposing on your vacation?"

"Only if you snore." I make a face like I ate something distasteful and shake my head. "Oh no. You do snore, don't you?"

"I do not," she shoots back, and picks up a pillow, ready to hurl it at me. Instead, she fluffs it and sets it on a nearby chair.

"All settled then." George nods. "I'll let you two get sorted out in your dome and I'll clean this up."

"Thanks, George," she says and we both head out into the late morning sunshine. She walks past me and goes to the Jeep to get her bags, and I hurry and walk to my dome, and hold the door open for her.

She looks less than impressed as she steps inside. I follow her in and nearly crash into her when she comes to an abrupt stop. "Do you like top or bottom?" she asks.

A noise I have no control over crawls out of my throat as I visualize her on the big comfy bed, me on top of her, beneath her, always inside her.

She spins, and her cheeks turn bright red. "I mean do you want the loft or do you prefer to sleep on ground level."

"I know what you mean."

She glares at me. "Then why did you make that sound...like I was asking about...about..."

"Sex?"

Her chest rises and falls quickly. "Yeah."

"I knew *you* weren't asking about sex, but you should probably know, I was thinking about it." I give a non-apologetic shrug. "What can I say, I'm a guy and you're a beautiful woman."

She blinks at me, like she's trying to understand the compliment, and if this woman isn't told she's beautiful every day, that's on those around her, not her. You know what else? She brought us here to have a relaxing vacation, yet I can't help but wonder when she last took a break. I'm guessing she doesn't. Maybe I'll do something about that this weekend. Maybe I'll turn this around and treat her to a little rest, or rather Wes, and relaxation. I grin, liking the idea of that.

She eyes me, her head angled, suspicion dancing on her face. "Why are you smiling like that?"

I reach out, and slide her back pack from her shoulder. "Because I'm on vacation, and I don't care if I'm on top or bottom. You pick."

Her brows furrow, and I guess she's trying to figure out what I'm up to. "It's really nice to sleep with the dome open so you can see the stars," she finally says. "You might like that."

I nod. "What's the benefit of being on ground level?"

She spins and points to the king-sized bed. "Look at that bed."

"Yeah, I think I might like that."

She laughs. "Couples probably need a cup and a string so they can hear and find each other."

I laugh at that, and she grins. "This is hardly roughing it. I'm sure they could find more modern technology and believe you me, I'd have no trouble finding you if you were in that bed."

Once again, her cheeks turn pink, and okay, maybe that was my purpose all along. Why not let her know how much I want her, why not lay it right out there, and see if she picks it up? We're consenting adults on vacation. So why not have some fun, and we can each go our own way when we're done. She gets to crawl into bed with an NHL player—that's what the girls want from us guys, right?—and I get a gorgeous fisherwoman who can totally handle life on her own, but that doesn't mean this weekend she has to.

She walks to the ladder and climbs it, and I can't seem to take my eyes off her ass. She makes a grunting sound as she drops her bag onto the bed, and starts to open the dome. Warm sunshine falls on us, and I take another look around, totally impressed that Charlie put this all together. Honestly, I've been camping, but I've slept on the ground. This place has a small kitchenette, a spacious bathroom, a big comfy bed and a reading chair. It's amazing, really, and tonight I'm anxious to get in the hot tub and enjoy the view of the ocean.

I walk over to the small fridge and pull it open to find it fully stocked. "Do George and Roxane take care of the place for you?"

"They do. Are you hungry?"

"Always."

She comes back down the ladder, and she has a pair of shorts and a T-shirt in her hands which kind of sucks because I like seeing her in my clothes. "Did you want to do the picnic lunch?" She narrows her eyes. "Jules and Rider haven't surfaced yet. Do you think we should check on them, see if they're interested in a hike and a picnic at the lighthouse?"

I grin at her. "They haven't had a lot of time to themselves since having Sophie, and this is sort of a honeymoon for them, so I say we leave them a note, and if their fridge is stocked like ours, I think they'll be fine."

She frowns, her eyes unsure. "I want to make sure they get the full experience."

I laugh, and it comes out sounding like a snort. "Believe me, they're getting the full experience."

She whacks me. "You know that's not what I meant."

"Wait," I tease. "You mean..." I jerk my thumb over my shoulder, and like an asshole, say, "What's going on next door isn't part of *my* full experience?"

Her head does some strange bobbing thing, which looks adorable. "Oh, you can have that all you want."

I angle my head and give her a second to continue, anxious to see where she's going with this. She reaches for my arm, flattens my fingers and shoves my palm to my chest. "Have at it, Hatfield."

I burst out laughing. "You're killing me, Charlie."

She disappears into the small bathroom, and I grab a bottle of water from the fridge and crack it. I take a long pull and try not to imagine her in here naked, but fail drastically. My pants have a bulge in them when she comes out, and dammit, she looks sexy in her frayed shorts and T-shirt. I turn so she doesn't see my bulge, but she goes straight to work pulling meats from the fridge.

"Let me help."

She waves me away. "I've got this."

"I'm not useless."

"I never said you were, but this trip is all about you. It's all about the guest experience."

"Okay, then. I want to help, and you can't say no because I'm the guest and it's what I want. The guest gets what the guest wants, right?"

She pauses and puts her hands on her hip. "Hmm, I guess when you put it like that, you're right. Okay, grab the bread and squirt on some mustard. You like mustard, right?" she asks, but my thoughts are already racing. If she's saying yes to me helping, because it's all about my experiences, what else will she say yes to when I pose the question like that? That makes me laugh because I only want her in my bed if she wants to be there, but what a fun way to make it happen.

She crinkles her nose, worry in her eyes. "Are you sure we shouldn't check on Jules and Rider?"

"Their place is locked up, Charlie. They basically have a do not disturb sign hung. They're fine, I promise, and it's really nice that you're taking such good care of my friends."

"I like them." She opens a package of sliced turkey, and exhales. "It's been nice hanging around Jules, actually. My friends have all moved away."

"That's what it's like here. It's hard to get anyone to stay. Sometimes I feel guilty that I didn't stay to work the farm, take it over when Mom and Dad retire. It's the way things are done, and without brothers and sisters, the farm either shuts down or it goes up for sale."

"There's no one else in your family who might want to run it?"

"My aunt and uncle on my Mom's side live in the city, and they both have government jobs. Their son, my cousin, is a total asshole who'd likely burn the farm down. Do you remember him?"

She looks up in thought. "I don't think so."

I shrug and squirt mustard onto the bread. "Yeah, why would you remember him? He's not from around here. He lives in the city, and doesn't visit for very long. Except for that one time... Speaking of the city, have you heard anything about the jobs yet?"

"No, not yet. Maybe they don't want me."

"It's their loss. Do they have any idea how creative and talented you are, and that you have great management skills?"

"You think so?" she asks, but she clearly already knows she does.

She layers the bread with meat, and adds on slices of cheese, and my stomach rumbles. She grins at me. "Should I make a couple more?"

I nod and she laughs, and I pull out more bread. We make the sandwiches, and she puts them in a cooler bag before putting it in her backpack. She tosses in some apples and water.

I tug on a ball cap, and she ties her hair back. "We need to lotion up. We don't want to burn."

"If we did, I bet you'd be prepared."

She gives me a sheepish grin as she tosses a bottle of lotion my way. "I may or may not have some aloe vera, and you should put on your swimsuit." She tugs her T-shirt away from her shoulder and exposes her bathing suit strap. "The water's cold, but we're picnicking on the beach so you might want to jump in if we get too hot."

Hell, the second I see her in that suit, I'll be jumping in. "Yeah, okay," I murmur and tug off my shirt to coat my body in lotion. Charlie stands there for one long second, staring at me. I clear my throat and her head lifts. She blinks rapidly as I grin at her, letting her know I'm well aware that she was just checking me out. She snatches the lotion and puts a generous amount on her arm. She turns from me, and takes off her T-shirt and her body does some strange contortionist move as she tries to lotion her back.

Biting back a grin, and working to keep my cock in lockdown, I take the lotion from her, and put my mouth close to her ear. She goes perfectly still, and telltale goosebumps break out on her neck, when I whisper, "Here, let me do that for you."

CHARLIE

The second his big, powerful hand lands on my back, touching me carefully, my entire body reacts, and I'm pretty sure he's well aware, and liking what his touch does to me.

I'd have no trouble finding you in that bed.

The back of my suit exposes most of my back, so he bends to get all my exposed skin and as his warm breath falls over me, those enticing words ring loud and clear in my brain. His hand moves up to rub my shoulders, a gentle massage that brings on a moan.

"You're tight, Charlie."

Oh gawd...

He presses into my muscles. "When was the last time you had a vacation?"

"Can't remember," I murmur, my voice low, almost drowsy... most definitely aroused.

He finishes, and his hands fall to his sides. "Would you mind doing me?"

Nope, wouldn't mind doing you at all, Wes.

As my thoughts wander, he presses the bottle into my hand, and I shake my head to clear it. Right, he means do his back. But maybe he doesn't. Maybe he's saying things that can be taken as sexual because it's what he wants. Cripes knows it's what I want too. Maybe he's simply feeling me out.

I turn and pour the lotion into my palm. I warm it and beginning with his broad shoulders, I work my way to the small of his back. His muscles ripple beneath my touch and I'm about two seconds from reaching around him, unbuttoning his pants, and checking out his equipment when a shuffling sound outside the dome reaches my ears.

"The mess is all cleaned up, Charlie," George says. "If you need anything else, just holler."

I step back, snatch up my T-shirt and pull it on. "Thanks, George. We're just lotioning up before we head out to the shore." Good Lord, why do I feel the need to explain that to George. Oh, probably because I weirdly feel like I got caught doing something naughty...dirty.

"You all have a good time, now. Don't be a stranger this weekend." He shuffles off, and I glance at Wes, take in those caramel eyes that any girl would get lost in.

"You go ahead and get changed. I'll see George to his truck," I say and dart outside like the dome is on fire. Jesus, I'm a mess. I really shouldn't be thinking about having sex with Wes, an NHL player who has a harem of bunnies—although Jules warned me not to believe everything I read. But he's a guy who hired my tour company, and I shouldn't be messing around with a customer, right? No matter how much my brain knows better, my body simply doesn't care.

I wave George off as he climbs into his truck, and turn to see Jules and Rider's dome all shut down. I smile. I like it when my guests love the little domes I built for the family business. It was a big investment, but one that's going to pay off.

"All set?"

I spin and come face to face with Wes, who has my backpack over his shoulder. "You have a little..." I reach out and smudge the streak of white lotion under his eye. His chest heaves as I touch him and I honestly have no idea how I'm going to spend the next few hours with him, sleep in the same dome as him without handing over my white panties in surrender.

"Get it?"

"Yeah," I say. He keeps pace beside me as we walk to the Jeep, and he jumps into the passenger's seat, which brings a smile to my face. I can't tell you how many times the guys I chauffer around insist on driving, like I don't know how to handle a simple Jeep. Wes seems quite content with me in charge. That makes me wonder, would he be like that in the bedroom or would he take the lead?

Which do I want more?

"I can't believe I grew up here and never once came to Brier Island."

I cast him a glance. "I love it here. It's so peaceful." We pass one car on the narrow road.

"If they could get the traffic under control, it'd be paradise."

I laugh at that. "Are you having fun so far?"

He points to his handsome face, and my gaze goes to his kissable lips. "Haven't smiled like this in a long time, Charlie."

"Yeah, how come?" I ask, hoping I'm not prying into something painful, but wanting to know more about him.

"Not a lot of downtime during the NHL season, and I worked my butt off to prove myself. Don't get me wrong, I'm grateful to be playing, it's a dream, but I really want to prove to the guys that I've earned my spot on the roster, you know?"

"I can understand that. Do they still call you the rookie?"

"Yeah." He laughs. "It's better than some of the things the guys are called. My buddy Declan is known as the Heartbreaker. He has this girl in his hometown, though. He says they're friends, but I think he wants more."

"That's a tough one."

"He goes home every Christmas, so maybe this year he'll finally stop being a chicken shit and do something about it. I know I would."

I eye him for a second. "You're saying if you want something, you go for it."

"That's right."

If he wants me, does that mean he's going to go for it?

God, I hope so.

"What about you?" he asks.

"I go after what I want," I say. There's no denying I want a piece of Wes, so why aren't I going for it? I guess maybe there is some small part of me that's worried about getting hurt. We're just so different. He's a big NHL star who got out of

Dodge as fast as he could. I'm a small-town girl, who doesn't want to leave, yet feel I have to. I should at least try a job in the city, right? That's what Mom wants. I'm not sure she thinks the sea is in my soul, or if she does, she still wants me to try other things, just to be certain what I want in life.

I turn the radio down, and jack the air conditioning. I take a fast peek at Wes' strong profile, and before I can stop myself, I ask, "Can I ask you a question?"

"Sure."

"Whatever happened with you and Breton, if you don't mind my asking?" I flick on my signal light and turn down the path leading to the beach. "I'm assuming it had to be something bad, if you had to grab the girl closest to you and kiss her to prove you weren't available."

"You mean I had to grab the most beautiful girl in the entire province."

I laugh at his playful words, but it falls flat when I note the seriousness on his face. "You thought I was a boy, Wes." Eyes full of want and need narrow, as he shifts to face me, making it very clear he now understands that I'm a girl.

"Listen, Mack," he teases. "You had your back to me, and—"

I put my fingers to his lips to stop him. "I'm just messing with you."

He grins, his look sheepish and adorable. "You're never going to let me live that down, are you?"

"Probably not."

"You like messing with me, huh?" His lips part and he takes my finger into his mouth. He licks it lightly, his heat seeping under my skin, and honest to God, he might as well be licking my clit, because that soft sweep of his tongue, the need it triggers, travels to the needy little spot between my legs and reminds me I haven't been touched in a long time.

"What...what are you doing?"

"You had a little mustard on your finger."

"Oh. Got it?"

"Yeah?"

I pull my finger out, and try to regulate my breathing. I stare out at the ocean, my thoughts a scattered mess when he clears his throat.

"Breton really hurt me."

I appreciate his honesty, but I had already figured that much out. "I'm sorry."

"It's okay. When I saw her at the Fish Shack, she talked about us hanging out, going for a drink. I'm not sure I could go through that again."

Ohmigod, he still loves her.

"You two were together most of high school, weren't you?"

"Yeah, then I got injured playing hockey, and I guess she thought she lost her ticket out of Digby."

"Wow, you think she was with you just to get out of here?"

"She dumped me, and started dating Sam Gilmore. Do you remember him?"

"Yeah, I know him well, actually. He called me Charlotte when he came into the store. He was always very nice to me." He gives me an odd look, like he doesn't quite understand what I'm talking about, and I say, "He's made quite the name for himself in the NFL."

"He did, and I always thought he was a nice guy. We always got along until Breton."

"Sounds like what happened wasn't his fault, though."

"No, you're right. She broke it off with me. It wasn't like they were cheating on me. She was free and clear when she went after him. He had no idea she was looking for a ticket out of here, and latched onto him because, with my injury, I'd be headed for a lifetime on the farm." He goes quiet, and it's easy to tell this trip down memory lane is a painful one. "When Sam left here, he broke up with Breton first. By that time, my knee injury had healed, much better than the doctors had first thought, and I was playing again. As soon as my future looked bright, she wanted to get back together."

My stomach clenches as I take in the hurt in his eyes. "That's shitty."

His throat makes a sound, a half laugh, half snort. "I never knew you were such a wordsmith, Baxter."

"There's a lot you don't know about me, but yeah, I think that's shitty," I say, my heart pinches tight. "Such a hurtful thing for her to do."

"You're right. That's why I kissed you."

"Pretending to be with me was to show her it was really over?"

"Something like that." I stare at him, and get the sense that he wants to say more about that.

"What?" I ask.

He opens his mouth, then closes it. When he finally speaks, he asks, "How come you're still single?" I eye him as he moves away from the subject of Breton. Is there another reason he kissed me? One he doesn't want me to know about. Is there more going on with him and Breton, and he doesn't want me to know?

"I dated a guy one summer. Thought we were in love, but it turned out we wanted different things." I shrug. "I haven't found a guy who wants the same things as I do." Honestly, I'm pretty sure I never will. Guys get out of Digby faster than our high-speed ferry. Slim pickings, to say the least.

"Maybe you'll find someone when you get to Toronto."

"Maybe," I say, and kill the ignition when I reach the beach. "Welcome to Pond Cove Beach and Nature Preserve."

He turns and a smile lights up his face. "Holy shit. This place is gorgeous." He scans the long length of empty beach. "And we have the entire place to ourselves." He gives me a wink full of mischief. "We can go skinny dipping."

"No, we can't." I laugh at his childlike enthusiasm, which is funny and kind of contagious. When was the last time I got to be a child? I honestly can't remember, but this weekend, maybe I can make up for that. Maybe I can be reckless and wild and forget about consequences. "Way down there you can see some seals. I am not flashing a bunch of seals."

"I don't think they'll mind."

"Okay then, I'm not flashing you, and you," I say pointing a finger at him and waving it up and down. "Keep your shorts on."

Or completely ignore me and take them off.

After all, I did just contemplate being reckless.

"We'll see." He laughs and jumps from the Jeep and hikes my bag over his shoulder.

"Want to eat first?"

He nods and rubs his stomach. "Yeah, but then I have to wait twenty minutes to go into the water."

"I think you'll be fine, plus I'm a certified lifeguard, so I'll save you." I lift my arm and show him my bicep muscle. "I might be small, but I'm strong."

"I watched you lift fifty-pound lobster bins. You don't have to convince me." He shakes his head, appreciation in his eyes. "You never cease to surprise me, Charlie Baxter."

What I do is considered unorthodox by most and I'm always judged, but Wes, well he's impressed with what I do, and everything in the way he looks at me, reminds me underneath it all, I'm a woman. Is he able to separate the girl from the seafarer?

I walk to the back of the Jeep and pull out a big plaid blanket. "Like I said, my mother wanted us to try everything at least once." I head toward the grassy area, and as we walk by a cluster of gorgeous yellow flowers, I stop to sniff them. "These are called Eastern Mountain Avens. Do you know there is only one other place in the world they grow?"

"Really?"

"Yup, New Hampshire." I cup one of the flowers. "These flowers act as solar collectors and follow the movement of the sun across the sky."

"You're making that up."

I laugh. "Now why would I make that up?"

"Because I think you like messing with me."

"That's true, but they really do follow the sun, and now you have a fact that is completely useless to you." He chuckles, and I straighten up and point to the highest hill. "Let's go eat there. We'll have a nice view of the ocean."

We hike up the hill and I lay the blanket out. Wes opens the backpack and takes out our lunch. We dig into our sandwiches and go quiet as pretty birds fly overhead. Once we're done eating, we both flop down on our backs to let our food digest before we brave the cold ocean.

I shut my heavy eyes. I stayed up too late last night, my mind on the guy beside me, and was up too early.

"Charlie?"

"Hmm."

"Whatever happened to your dad?"

"He left when I was seven."

"That's shitty. See I'm a wordsmith too. But I'm really sorry."

"It's okay. He and Mom wanted different things in life. He wanted to live in the city, she wanted to stay here and work in the fishing industry. She gave it up early in the marriage and went to the city, but it wasn't for her. They came back here, and this life wasn't for him. They both grew up here, like us, but he needed out, and she needed to stay." I angle my head to see him and he's watching me carefully, thoughtfully.

"That's why it's important for you, then." His eyes narrow, like he's putting pieces of a puzzle together. "You know, to be with someone who wants the same things."

"Yeah."

I close my eyes, and we both go quiet. The next thing I know I'm waking up, confused. Where the hell am I? My brain kicks into gear, and that's when I realize one arm and one leg are thrown over Wes.

"Ohmigod," I say, and I'm about to pull away but he holds me to him. "Why didn't you wake me?"

"You were tired. It's no big deal." He brushes my hair from my face and smiles. My heart misses a beat as his warm gaze moves over my face. "You don't snore, but you kick around a lot in your sleep."

"I'm so sorry."

"It's not a big deal, not out here in this wide-open space, but if you're in that small bunk bed above me, you might hurt yourself, or worse, fall overboard and land in my bed."

I take in his playful look, the mischief dancing in his gorgeous eyes. "What...what are you suggesting?"

"That maybe you should just start out in my bed. Either way, you're probably going to wake up in it."

Did Wes just come right out and ask me to sleep with him?

9

WES

"We need to get you warmed up," I say to Charlie as she continues to shiver, her body shaking as she drives us back to our dome. I reach out and rub her arm to create heat with friction, yet her teeth continue to rattle. If I had it my way, I'd take her into the back seat and use my body to warm her properly, not to mention my mouth or my cock. My dick twitches, liking that idea.

"How are you not cold?" she asks through chattering teeth as she casts me a suspicious glance. "You have zero body fat, and that water was below freezing."

"You think I have zero body fat?" I ask and she rolls her eyes. "For the record, I am cold, and that water was a balmy minus two at the most." It's a fib. I'm not cold. I'm downright hot. Seeing her in her sexy one-piece bathing suit heated the blood in my veins, and not even the cold Atlantic waters could douse the fire singeing my skin. I peel my T-shirt off and hand it to her. "Pull this on."

"I don't believe you," she grumbles. "You're not even shivering. Maybe all that muscle keeps you warm."

"You think I have a lot of muscle?" I tease, just to get a reaction out of her and she rewards me with a shake of her head.

"It's a simple observation. Save your charm for the whales. It's lost on me."

I laugh at that and take the wheel from the passenger seat, enjoying the easiness between us. While I want to spend time with my friends, I'm grateful for this time alone with Charlie. I like getting to know her. I steer as she tugs on my big shirt and hugs herself.

"What about being a gentleman? Is that lost on you too?" I ask.

"No, I really appreciate the shirt." She flashes me a grateful smile and my heart skips a couple beats. She is so freaking sweet and gorgeous, and I don't even think she knows it. I like that about her. She's a natural beauty, doesn't have to work at it, and is less than interested in impressing me, even though everything she does is highly impressive.

"I think I'm going to have to get into the hot tub," she mumbles.

"Yeah, me too."

She casts me a quick glance. "You're not cold."

"I am." I hug myself. "Freezing." She rolls her eyes at me and continues to drive. I turn the air conditioning to heat, and roll my window up as a breeze washes in. "Better?"

"I don't think I'll ever get warm again."

Her teeth continue to chatter as she drives and a few minutes later we pull up to our dome. Nothing is too far on this island.

"Come on," I say, and circle the car, and put her under my arm as I lead her to the hot tub, which is nestled in between domes one and two, so all guests can enjoy it. "I shouldn't have coaxed you into the water. My bad."

"I wanted to go in. Besides," she casts me a fast glance. "It's my job to ensure my guests are having fun, remember?"

"So you'd do anything to make it a good guest experience, huh?" I ask, a leading question, I know.

She eyes me, like she knows exactly what's going through my lust-rattled brain. "Define anything?"

I grin at that, and we reach the wooden deck, and I flip the lid to the hot tub. Warm steam rushes out and clouds the air. Charlie quickly peels my shirt, then her shirt and her shorts off, her bathing suit underneath and lets out a loud sigh when she slides into the heated water.

"Sooo nice," she moans and her moan of pleasure wraps around my cock and squeezes tight.

I follow her in, and the water rises as I sit next to her and adjust the bubbles in the jets. "You went all out on these domes. How long have you had them?"

"This is my second summer. I'm pretty booked up. This was the only weekend they were free. You got lucky."

"I like getting lucky," I tease, my voice holding all kinds of sexual innuendos. I move a bit closer, and our legs touch. A little sound catches in her throat and my cock thickens even more. Having her wrapped around me when she slept...Jesus, her body was warm, soft, so damn enticing, I nearly rubbed one out while she slept quietly. If I don't do something soon about the need building inside me, I fear I might rupture something.

"Warm?" I ask.

"Getting there."

I lift my arms and brace them on the side of the tub, one going around her back. She angles her head my way, her blue eyes a shade deeper. I curl a strand of her hair around my finger, and give a little tug to tilt her head back, and part her lush lips.

"If a customer wanted to touch you like this," I say, unraveling her hair so I can brush my thumb over her shoulder. "Would you let him, you know to give him the best possible experience?"

Her breathing changes, becomes a bit deeper. She goes quiet and I suspect one of two things are going through her head. One, she's contemplating on whether to give me a good nut punch, or two, she's thinking about playing along, to see where this game takes us.

"I suppose," she says breaking the quiet. "I wouldn't want anyone walking away from here...unsatisfied."

Jesus Christ, she's playing along.

"Word of mouth is a big thing," she explains.

Mouth...big thing. Yeah, I can work with that.

I move closer, and run my finger over the top of her bathing suit, lightly caressing the delicate skin on her chest, the tips of my fingers close to the swell of her breasts but not quite touching.

"If a customer wanted to touch you like this, what would you do?"

"I guess I'd let him," she says, answering quickly this time. "If that's what makes him happy."

Taking my chances, I let my hand drop, and ever so lightly brush my thumb over her hard nipple. She takes a fast breath, a moaning sound catching in her throat as she shifts in her seat, arching into my touch.

"If he wanted to touch you here, you'd agree?"

"I'd agree," she murmurs. My cock throbs in my swim shorts, and I'm about to ask her to touch me in return when laughter reaches our ears, and I pull my hand back and put a small measure of distance between us when Jules and Rider come around the corner. Jules goes completely still when she sees us.

"Oh, shoot. We're interrupting."

"No, no, it's okay," Charlie says quickly. If it were up to me, I'd tell them to take a long hike, but Charlie is in charge here, so I shut my mouth. Later however... "We're just warming up because we were crazy enough to go into the ocean." She pats the water. "Join us."

"Are you sure?" Rider asks, no doubt aware that I'm sporting a raging hard on by the way my face is twisted in torture.

I wave them over, because it's what Charlie wants, and what she wants, she gets—at least with me. "Get in here." I put my mouth close to Charlie's ear. "Later tonight, I want to talk more about my guest experience."

Her chest rises and falls and she sinks deeper into the water.

"Sorry we didn't join you on your adventure," Jules says.

"As long as you're having a good time, that's all that matters. Tomorrow I have a hike planned and I'd love it if you'd join, but understand if you just want to rest."

"We're having the best time, and we definitely want to hike." She smiles at me. "I'm so glad you booked this for us, Wes." It's funny, Jules was one of the first wives to take me under her wing, and now they all treat me like their little brother. I can't deny that I love it. Like I said, I always wanted a big family and I love being a part of Rider and Jules', and Charlie here, that's the icing on the cake, but this is just temporary. I mean I know what's missing from my life, and I'm not saying I might want more with this beautiful woman.

I'm not saying I don't, either...

"For dinner, I'm barbecuing steaks," Charlie says, bringing my thoughts back. "And then we can have a bonfire. I have everything we need to make s'mores."

"You go all out for your guests, don't you?" Jules lays her head back, and adds, "This is all amazing."

"She definitely goes above and beyond," I say and slide my hands into the water. I lightly brush her outer thigh. She takes another quick breath, but Jules and Rider are resting their heads back, staring at the blue sky. She glances at me and telegraphs a message to cut it out, but I smile innocently at her and move my hand until I'm touching her inner thigh. Her throat makes a sound as she swallows, and something comes over her, a change, and the next thing I know, she presses her hand to my swollen dick, and I damn near jump out of the hot tub in surprise.

She grins at me, as if to say that two can play that game, and she's right. Two *can* play that game and tonight I plan to play, all night long.

"I'm starting to wrinkle," Charlie says, and lifts herself up. "You guys stay and enjoy. I need to get dressed and start to get things ready for dinner."

"I'll help." I make a move to jump up and she shakes her head.

"No, you don't have to do that."

"But I want to, which means you have to let me, or I'll walk away unsatisfied, and maybe even leave a bad review."

She puts a hand on her hip. "You wouldn't do that."

"You don't know what I'd do," I tease. "With the right motivation..."

She brushes her hair away from her flushed cheeks. "If you really want to help..."

"I want," I say, leaving no mystery about what it is I really want from her.

"Come on then." She heads toward my dome, and I can't help but stare at her ass. Jules makes a happy, squealing sound as I follow Charlie. Inside the dome, she goes up the ladder and comes back down with dry clothes. I surf through my bag to pull out jeans and a clean shirt as she darts to the small washroom to change.

I slip into dry clothes, and she comes out, looking warm, sexy, so inviting, I nearly bite off my tongue. "The steaks are in my dome," she says. "You don't have to help if you don't want to."

"I want to. I'll get the barbecue lit." I pull a bottle of wine from the counter. "You can sit, drink wine, and order me around."

"But—"

"It's what I want."

She eyes me. "You want to do all the cooking, while I drink wine? How does that make sense? This is your vacation." She pokes my chest, and I bring her finger to my mouth to lick it. When she casts me a questioning glance, I lie and say, "Mustard."

She pulls her finger back and I open the wine and pour a generous amount into a glass. I fill another for Jules, and grab two beers, for Rider and me.

"That's a lot of alcohol. You're not trying to get me drunk and take advantage of me later, are you?"

I step closer, my body crowding hers, and hand her glass over. A little sound flutters from her lips, a telltale sign she might want that. "No, Charlie. When I take advantage of you later, I want you wide awake and fully aware."

As pink flushes her cheeks, she takes a big sip of wine, and I reach out and brush the corner of her mouth where a droplet lingers. I slide my finger into my mouth for a taste, and when I moan, she gulps.

"I...I should get the...uh...the beef, I mean the meat. Steak. Yeah, I should get the steaks."

I grin, as she stumbles over her words, clearly as aroused as I am. "Is that what you want?" I ask.

"It's not about what I want, Wes. It's about what my guests want."

"This guest wants you, on that bed, your legs spread wide open so I can do dirty things to your body."

"Oh, God."

"But the guest experience is important to you and I know you want to make it nice for Jules and Rider, and I appreciate and respect that, so how about this. We cook up a meal, and have that bonfire you planned, then later, I want you in my bed, where it's going to be all about the things *you* want. Dirty things. That's what this customer wants."

Sexual tension surrounds us, takes up space between our bodies as her mouth opens and closes. I step to the side to allow her to pass. As she walks on shaky legs, I lean into her and murmur, "You can think about that for the rest of the evening, and when we're back here, when I have you naked and on the bottom—yeah, tonight I want the top—I want you to tell me everything you want."

Wine in hand, she disappears out the door and I grin. I honestly can't remember the last time I wanted anyone so badly. I snatch up the beer and wine and walk to the hot tub.

"Oh, you are too sweet," Jules says as she graciously accepts the glass. I click bottles with Rider and we both take a mouthful.

"Did I see Charlie coming out of your dome?" Jules asks.

"Yeah, an animal destroyed her mattress and I offered to share my dome."

Jules grins. "How very Canadian of you."

I glance at Rider, who has caution and worry on his face. He knows my background, and what really went down with Breton. His warning look isn't necessary. What's going on here between Charlie and me is just physical attraction. I really do know better than to fall for a hometown girl, seeking a way out. I can't—won't—go down that road again. As I think about that, there's a part of me that says she wouldn't come with me even if I wanted her to, and don't even ask me to explain the knot that brings to my stomach.

"Steaks will be ready in about half an hour. Meet us at the barbecue area." I take another drink of my beer, and head toward the barbecue, where I find Charlie making up a salad at the picnic table.

I eye the big steaks as I step up to her and put my hands on her waist and my mouth near her ear, wanting her as aroused as I am. A hard quiver goes through her, but I know she's no longer cold.

"Looks delicious," I murmur. My cock thickens and presses against her back, and I don't bother to hide it. "I can't wait to eat."

"Steaks shouldn't take too long to get ready."

"Babe, it's not the steak I want in my mouth, it's you."

CHARLIE

onight has been the most insane night of my entire life, and no I'm not exaggerating. Every time I think about the things Wes said to me—that he wants me to tell him what I want—my body burns with a need that is foreign but thrilling. Honest to God, the entire night has been like one long drawn-out foreplay session, leaving my body on hyperdrive and my brain buzzing like a swarm of bees.

I turn to find him staring at me, that knowing little grin on his face. My God, I'm not all that experienced in bed, and never have I told a man what I wanted sexually. Yes, we're playing a game here, one that involves guest satisfaction, but the truth is, out on this island it's like we're living in an alternate reality, a dreamlike state of constant arousal.

Over the course of the evening, during dinner and around the bonfire, there was enough electricity arcing between the two of us to ignite the trees and burn down the entire island, and not even the surrounding ocean could extinguish the flames. But to tell him what I want...

Do I dare?

Do I dare not?

Right now, as I sit on a log, roasting another marshmallow—maybe I'm stalling—it's all I can do to keep my hands from shaking, and don't even get me started on breathing. Cripes, filling my lungs is a goddamn chore. Never in my life have I experienced anything like this. Everything about me is constricted, jittery, so freaking aroused, I'm sure if I shift on this log the wrong way, or the right way, I'm going to get myself off. Ooh, now there's an idea. Maybe I should take the edge off to calm myself down before I explode and blast off into space. Is Wes as messed up as I am? Then again, it's not like it's been years since he's been touched.

"I can't remember the last time I had this much fun," Jules says, putting her hand over her mouth as she yawns. "But I have to call it a night."

"So soon?" I say and catch the smirk on Wes' face. He knows what's going on with me. He knows that I know, the second we're alone he's going to ravish me, and I want that, I really do. I'm also just a little afraid. I've never been devoured—never had a man look at me quite the way he's been looking at me all night. It worries me. The truth of the matter is, he's proving to be a really sweet guy, a guy who cares about what I want, and while I'm eager to mess around, I can't have him mess with my heart. He's here on vacation, a guy who couldn't wait to get out of this town. I might soon be moving to Toronto, as much as I hate that idea. I also can't forget that I'm pretty sure he's still in love with his ex. Maybe what he's doing with me is simply to make her jealous, to get her back. Maybe he's past the hurt and ready to start new with her. Really, I don't know and right now my brain is in no shape to puzzle things out.

"We want to get a good night sleep before the hike tomorrow." Rider stands and pulls his wife up. "Do you need any help getting the fire out?" he asks.

"Nope." Wes pokes the burning logs with a stick, and he's not only stoking the flames in the pit, but he's also stoking the flames burning through me. My God, just watching him standing there, his body all power and muscles, so damn fit and fine, it's enough to turn a girl into a bumbling idiot.

I blow on the marshmallow and take a bite of the sweet gooeyness, and as we all say good night, I hold my stick out to Wes. He steps closer, crouches beside me, his presence completely overwhelming me as he opens his mouth. Trying to keep my hands from shaking, I feed him the sweet treat, and my nipples pinch tight, as I imagine him taking them into his mouth, instead. He moans, deep and sexy, and that's the sound I want to hear when he has me naked—because yeah, we're definitely getting naked at some point.

"Delicious," he murmurs. "Everything tonight was great, Charlie." His smile is warm, sincere, and his voice is suddenly soft, but behind it all, I sense the beast stirring, the wild animal waiting to be untethered. Damned if I don't want to snap that leash and let him have his way with me, even though I'm a girl who never really hands herself over.

I stand and brush my hands over my jeans. "I guess we should call it a night too, huh."

"The night is just beginning, babe."

My gaze flies to his, and he takes a step closer, crowds me, and he lifts his hand, puts it on the side of my face.

"You're not tired?" I ask, and curse the quiver in my voice. God, there is no hiding my desire when I'm around him.

"No. Are you?"

I gesture with my head, and nod to nowhere in particular. "I had that nap."

He grins. "I remember the nap." A beat of silence, and then, "Have you thought about it?"

My body burns as he asks the question that's been racing through my brain all night.

What do I want?

"Hose," I say.

A chuckle rumbles in his throat. "I'm working with some great equipment, babe. But I can't give you a hose."

"Ohmigod, no. I didn't mean that." Mortified, heat crawls up my neck. I cover my face with my hands and pray for the ground to open up and swallow me whole. This prolonged foreplay is zapping my brain cells one by one.

His soft laugh curls around me. "I know. I was just messing with you."

I whack him. "Jerk."

"I'll make it up to you. I promise." He glances around. "Where is this hose you speak of?"

"I can do it."

He captures my elbow, and pulls me close, close enough that his thickening cock indents my stomach, and for a second, I can't help but think he's not as calm as he's trying to portray.

"I know you can, but I can too." He brushes my hair from my face. "And when I'm done, I'm going to do all the dirty things to you, Charlie."

"Hose...over there," I blurt out, and he grins at my enthusiasm. I take in the quirk of his lips, and my own tingle with the urgency to kiss him again.

"You go on in, and I'll take care of this."

While I'm not used to anyone doing things for me—heck, I've been independent my whole life—I nod eagerly. In the dark, the path lit only by the bonfire, I walk like a drunken sailor to my dome, or rather Wes' dome. My stupid legs are all wobbly and my heart is racing so hard, I think I might break a rib. I step into the dome and his scent is all over the place. I stand there for a brief second and glance around, my gaze landing on that big, comfy king-sized bed.

What do I do? Do I crawl in it and strike a sexy pose? That thought brings a maniacal laugh to my throat. I wear rubber boots and coveralls—the opposite of the girls he gravitates toward. What the hell do I know about being sexy? The smell of billowing smoke reaches my nostrils as Wes douses the fire and I hurry up the ladder to root my pajama shorts and T-shirt from my bag. I tug them on, and glance out the unzipped roof to admire the stars glimmering in the velvet backdrop.

Footsteps announce Wes' arrival, and he secures the door behind him. He makes a trip to the bathroom, and when he comes out, I sit quietly on my bed, trying not to breathe, or make a sound. I have no idea what I'm doing. I want this. I want him. I'm just a jittery mess of arousal, and maybe in the back of my mind, I'm worried that once I've been with a guy like him, it'll ruin me for any other man. He is after all, an NHL superstar with a harem of women.

That means he should know how to please you, so tell him what you want already.

"Is the loft where you want me to do all the dirty things to you, Charlie?"

OMG. His words are crude, and sexy all at the same time and I make a gasping sound, surprised by how much I like his deep tenor, the way he gets right to the point.

"I...uh..."

He walks to the end of the ladder. "There is no way you're leaving this place unsatisfied."

"It's supposed to be the other way around," I croak out, and have no idea why I said that. But what kind of man comes to a place like this, where his satisfaction is my utmost importance, and turns it around on me.

A very considerate one... Why though? Why is he being so considerate? This is the guy that teased me relentlessly years ago.

"Maybe so, but this guest wants to take you six ways to Sunday, and what a guest wants he gets, right?" I crawl to the end of the bunk and peek at him. He grins up at me. "Are you coming down or am I coming up there to get you?"

I shift, and put one foot on the ladder, and can almost feel his eyes drilling into my ass. As I reach the bottom step, big hands circle my waist and set me on the floor. I slowly turn, and my pulse jumps at the intense way he's staring at me.

This man is going to eat me alive. But more importantly, I'm going to let him. I take in the leaves on his clothes, the soot from the fire.

"You're all dirty," I say.

"You don't know the half of it," he warns and slides one big hand around my neck. Shivers race down my spine as he angles his head and presses his lips to mine, and just like that, I lose myself in his kisses. His tongue meets mine, and he tastes me, takes me, and groans into my mouth. Excitement that I can do this to him dances in my nervous stomach.

His hand falls from the back of my neck, and he gathers my hands and secures them behind my back, holding them in place with one big hand and my pulse jumps. He eyes me. "Don't like that?"

"I...I...it's different."

"You've taken care of yourself for a very long time now, haven't you?"

"Yes."

"In the bedroom too, right?"

"Right." Why not admit it. His goal is to pleasure me and I'd be a fool not to be honest.

He runs his fingers down my neck, and slides it down my side, caressing the outer edge of my breast. My entire body quakes. "Are you afraid of me?"

"No." Not entirely true. This man is proving to be kind and sweet and I might be a little afraid of growing feelings for him. I can't do that. We live in different worlds, and I'm pretty sure his heart still belongs to his ex.

He studies my face, and after a long moment, he says, "If I asked you to put yourself in my hands and trust me, do you think you could do that?"

I gulp.

He exhales, his warm breath flutters against my skin, a mixture of marshmallow and minty toothpaste. "Better question is, do you want that? I want you to be honest with yourself. Out here, in the middle of nowhere, can we just be two country kids with nothing to hide?"

His voice snags, and something in the way he called us two country kids, like we're more alike than not, strikes a chord in me. Is that who he wants to be when he's with me? A small town farmer, over an NHL superstar?

I glance at the big bed behind me, and my brain settles, liking that idea. Suddenly ready and eager for this to happen, I begin with, "You asked me what I wanted."

He stares at my mouth, "I did."

Here goes nothing, and everything. "From the second you walked into the Lobster Pound, I wanted you, Wes Hatfield. I wanted you naked. On top of me, beneath me, in front of me and even behind. I want to do things with you that I've never done with anyone and I want you to do things to me that I've never heard of." A big breath and then, "I want your mouth on me, your fingers inside me. I want you to fuck me until reality is no longer in my vocabulary."

He grins. "I love a girl who knows what she wants."

"It's what I want, while we're here on this island."

"You love it here, don't you?"

"It's my Disney world," I say with a laugh. "Reality doesn't exist, just fantasy, so while we're here, we can live in that fantasy," I say, needing to clarify where we stand. I don't want him to think I want more when this is over.

Do you want more, Charlie?

Maybe, but I'm not the kind of girl he goes for, and while we're here, hiding out from the real world, we can enjoy each other, but I'm not the kind of girl seen on his arm. Plus, I'm pretty sure he's still hung up on Breton.

"Fantasy weekend, I got it," he murmurs in understanding as he reaches down, and touches the hem of my pajama shorts. A few loose strings tickle my inner thighs, and a hard quake overtakes my body. "The second you turned around in the Lobster Pound and I realized it was you, Charlie, I wanted my mouth all over you. Everything about you turns me on, especially the coveralls and rubber boots."

I grin at that, not sure I believe him, but hey, we all have our fetishes, and this guy must be into seafarers. I gesture with a nod. "Those rubber boots are in the boat. Want me to go get them?"

"Later," he growls, and the next thing I know, he's devouring me with his mouth and picking me up. I wrap my legs around him, and his raging hard cock presses against my center. I have no idea what I'm getting into with farm boy here, but I can't wait to find out.

He backs up, and when we hit the bed, he sets me on it. I lean back and his gaze rakes over me, ravenous, wild, and my entire body quakes with excitement.

"Why don't you get naked and show me those home-grown muscles, Hatfield," I say.

The corner of his mouth twitches. "Is that what you want?"

"I want to see your body."

He reaches over his back and tears off his T-shirt and once again the sight leaves me in awe. A strangled noise crawls out of my throat, and deep between my legs, I grow wetter.

"Your turn."

I straighten up, and grip the hem of my pajama shirt to peel it over my head. I sit there before him in my white lacy bra, and his gaze slides downward. "Fuck, yeah," he whispers.

"You like them now, huh?" I ask. Back in the day he teased me relentlessly.

His face scrunches. Does he not remember teasing me? "Yeah, I fucking like them." As if to prove it, he drops to his knees, slides his hand around my back, and with a single flick, undoes my bra. It falls and his eyes darken as he lightly brushes the outer edges of my breast. I've never had a man worship my body quite the way Wes is right now.

His head lifts and he's almost in a dreamlike state when he says, "I'm going to take such good care of these." I stare at him, not sure how to respond to that, so instead I say nothing and he draws one hard nipple into his mouth, and suck so hard, I feel the pressure deep between my legs.

"God, yes," I say and cup the back of his head to hold him to me. "That is..." My breathing changes as he switches tactics and slowly swirls his tongue over my nipple, soaking my flesh, and turning me on even more. The second he touches my sex, I know I'm going to go off like a nuclear explosion.

"You taste so good," he murmurs around my hard nipple. "I can't wait to taste you here." He grips my thighs, widens my legs and slides that handy hand of his between them, toying with the edge of my pajama shorts. He tugs on the cuff, widening the space between my leg and the slip of material to accommodate his fingers.

Yes, please...

With nothing in the world existing but the two of us, I shift a little to give him better access and his lips curl. "So needy." I move my hips, begging without words for him to touch me, and he obliges, sliding one finger into the gap, and brushing my sex through my panties. "You're on fire," he growls.

"I know." I'm not about to lie, not when I'm drenched and quivering and desperate for his touch. If he has a change of heart I might melt into a puddle, right at his feet.

"It's been...a long time."

He nods, and I run my hands over his back, loving all his hard muscles—born from hours working a farm. I like that about him. I like that he's not afraid of hard work, and the thoughts of him in rugged work clothes on the farm turns me on. Jeez, now who's the one with the fetishes?

Without even taking my shorts down, he pushes a hand inside and strokes my clit. I nearly leap off the bed as that first delicious touch sends pleasure rocketing through me. There's something about the way he's sneaking into my pajamas, stroking me with my clothes still on that makes it deliciously dirty—like we're back in high school, using our hands to get each other off behind the bleachers where we could be caught any second. No, it's not something I've done, but admittedly thought about. Maybe I really am living out many lost years with him.

Down on his knees, he rocks into me, mimicking the action of fucking, and I crave to touch his cock as it aches for relief. Dammit, I want to make him feel this good too, with every part of my body, starting with my mouth.

I'm about to reach down when he gives my shoulders a push and I fall to my back. He smiles at me, but I can't smile back. Nope, not when he's sliding a thick finger into my hot sex, stroking so delightfully deep, and hitting the hot bundle of nerves my ex could never find. I moan and fist the bedding, my head going from side to side as heat races to my core. Pleasure centers in my sex and my sex muscles tighten around his thick, deft finger.

"Wes," I cry out. Ohmigod, I'm going to come. I have never climaxed so fast in my life and as much as I want to let go, I don't want this to be over. I try to hold off. I bite down on my lip but he adds pressure to my clit, determined to push me over the edge.

"This is just to take the edge off, babe," he whispers. "You need this." I blink up at him and his jaw is tight, the muscles rippling. He's a hot mess, like me, desperate for it too, which makes me wonder just how long it's been for him. "Then I'll slow things down, because I want to play with you until the sun comes up, no rush, no hurry. I just want to take my time and fuck every inch of you."

"Oh, God, yes."

"Good, then why don't you come all over my finger, then later when I take you again, it will be with my mouth. The only thing that's going to douse the fire inside me is your cum on my tongue, babe." I take a deep, labored breath. "You want that, don't you?"

"God, yes, I want that."

He continues to finger fuck me, long strokes that take me to the edge. I whimper and cry and he changes the rhythm, moving a little faster.

"Yeah, just like that," he says as my sex flutters around his finger. "Now that I have you where I want you, I'm going to do all the things to you. Things you never even knew you wanted."

And just like that my body lets go, and my mouth drops open as a powerful climax crashes over me. Pleasure pulses between my legs as I coat his finger and my panties in my hot juices. I chant his name, as he stays on his knees, his finger inside me as I continue to clench around him. My brain buzzes as the sound of his zipper releasing reaches my ears and thrills me.

I finally stop clenching, and he ever so slowly removes his finger and stands. He licks his finger like it's a goddamn ice cream cone and groans with pleasure. Heart racing, I glance up at him, as once he's done tasting me, he tugs his shorts off, and gifts me with a view of his gorgeous, thick cock.

"You lied to me, Wes."

His body stiffens, and he angles his head as his eyes narrow, worry lingering in the depths. "I have no reason to lie to you, Charlie."

"Then why did you lead me to believe you didn't have a hose?"

WES

I laugh at her joke as she stares at my dick with awe and hunger as I take it into my palm and stroke it. I hate that it's been so long for her, that she hasn't been pleasured in a long time, but there's another side of me, a barbaric jealous side that is now alive and rearing, wanting to lay claim to the woman below me. It's fucking insane. I can't be falling for her. We barely know each other, and I can't forget that scowl on her face when I walked into the Lobster Pound, the way she so easily dismissed me like I'd wronged her. It still haunts me. Then again hate and sex, much like love and sex, are two different things.

I tug my dick harder and a growl rumbles in my throat. Blue eyes slowly lift and meet mine, her hair a mess of curls around her gorgeous, flushed face. Honestly, I'd like nothing better than to stay in this dome for the entire weekend, repeatedly bringing her to climax. Not just for her, but for me too. Bringing her pleasure, taking care of her needs and watching her put herself in my hands does the weirdest things to me.

"Has the guest experience been living up to your expectations?" she asks, but behind the joke I detect a hint of worry. It's true, she's different from the women I've been photographed with, the few bunnies I have slept with. But she's so much more. She's everything a man would want, and then some.

Careful, dude. This is just sex.

"Far better than expected," I say honestly, and her face softens into a smile that wraps around my heart and squeezes tight. Wow, I really like this girl.

"Is there anything I can do to make it extraordinary?" she asks, her voice a deep, breathless whisper full of arousal. Jesus, I like the way I affect her. "Your satisfaction is my top priority, you know."

I dip my head. "While I appreciate that, right now your satisfaction is my top priority."

She bites her bottom lip, her lips quirking at the corners. "Right, I understand that's what the guest wants. That doesn't mean you're walking out of here without a smile on your face, too, Wes."

She sits up, and positions her mouth near my cock and as I stroke from base to tip, and her moan of want thrills me. She reaches out and runs her thumb over my crown, dipping into my pre-cum. She brings it to her mouth and moans as she licks, and it's all I can do not to shoot down her throat. I fear I'm going to climax as fast as she did, but I love how needy she was. How much she wanted me. Me, the farm boy, not the NHL player. I'm right about that, aren't I?

"What I want is to put my cock inside your tight, hot pussy, and fuck you until the cows come home."

She breathes faster, but her eyes are somber, deadpan serious. "You have cows?"

I can't help but laugh at that. "Yes, of course I have cows. I'm from farm country."

"These cows." she blinks rapidly. "Are they lost?"

I laugh at her playfulness. My God, there is so much more to this girl. "Well no, 'until the cows come home' is a saying."

"Yeah, I know. I've heard it before. Just messing with you." She glances at my cock. "Now that I know what kind of equipment the farm boy is working with…" She crooks her finger. "Come here."

"You ready for me, Charlie? Ready to let me fuck you until you explode all over my cock?" A breathy sound rushes from her lips, and heat moves into her cheeks. She loves the dirty talk, and I'm not even sure she knew that about herself before tonight. "I'm going to fuck you so hard, put so much cum inside you, tomorrow on our hike, it'll be dripping out of you all day."

I rub my cock a little harder, and every muscle in my body tightens with need. We both of course know what I'm saying won't happen. I plan to use a condom. I don't take chances, and even if a girl tells me she's on the pill, I still use protection. I've seen guys get trapped, and I always have to keep my wits about me. What this is, it's just dirty talk to fire her up. Hell, it fires me up too. "You'll feel me, Charlie, and every time you do, I want you to think about what I'm going to do to you when our hike is over and I get you back in this bed. Or better yet, maybe I'll find a private spot in the woods to take you during our hike, a spot where we can get really dirty."

"Oh, God, Wes."

Her hand slides between my legs and she takes my balls into her palm. A light massage that forces me to grind my back teeth to keep it together. She leans forward, opens her mouth and poises her tongue under my crown.

"Holy fuck." I grip her hair to hold her head back an inch, afraid if she licks me I'll lose it. But her intent isn't to lick me. Nope, it's to catch the droplet spilling from my slit. Jesus Christ, that has to be the sexiest thing I've ever seen. The drop falls to her waiting tongue, and with no air left in my lungs, I let go of my dick, and drop back to my knees. Disappointment flashes in her eyes.

"I want..."

"It's about what I want, though," I remind her. "And right now, I want your legs around my neck and my mouth on your pussy. I need to taste you, Charlie. I need you to come all over my face."

"Right, sorry," she whispers, her voice quivering. "If that's what you want, then I have to oblige."

I grin at her, and love this sexy game we're playing. I also love the dreamy look in her eyes. I've seen it in the pictures hanging at her family home, and now I'm seeing it again. I'm not sure what she was dreaming of in those photos but right now, it's clear she's visualizing my mouth on her everywhere, wanting that every bit as much as I do.

"Yeah, sorry, but you do have to oblige." I chuckle at our use of sorry. Could we be any more Canadian?

She lays back and I make quick work of her shorts. I breathe in her scent and throw her pajama shorts toward my bag because no way is she getting those back. I'm not really sure why I need a souvenir from this trip, but I do. I dip my head to breathe her in and know without a doubt she's going to be the sweetest thing I've ever tasted.

I lightly circle her sensitive clit, and she writhes beneath me, reaching above her head to grip the pillow like she's hanging on for the ride. I put her legs around my neck and I stick my tongue out, and she lifts her hips. She moans as she rubs her hot pussy against the tip of my tongue.

"More," she cries out, but I only allow her to reach the soft tip of my tongue. She moans and rips at the sheets, needy, delirious, just the way I want her. Yeah, I can't be the only one this crazed right now.

"I'm right here, babe." I lap at her. "Come take what you need."

She cries out and reaches for my head. She grips my hair and pulls me to her sweet cunt, and smashes my lips to her sex and I eat at her like a man starved, craving something he never knew he needed until he tasted it. I crawl onto the bed and reach up to shift her higher. In a fast move, I flip, and take her with me, until she's on top. Her knees go around my head and she sits up, takes her breasts into her hands.

God, she's beautiful.

I hold her hips and she tries to push down onto my face, but I don't let her, instead, I hold her high, let her hover above my face, and lick at her clit, light soft strokes that drive her wild, judging by the way she's throwing her head back and moaning.

"What do you need?" I ask.

"I need to fuck your mouth," she says without hesitation.

Sweet Jesus, I love when she says things like that to me. "Ride me, babe. Rub your hot cunt all over my face until you come. I want to taste every last drop."

A hard quake goes through her body as I release the hold on her body and let her settle on my face. She puts her hands on her thighs, spread wide around my head and rolls her hips, using my face to get herself off and I fucking love it. She rocks against me, and my fingers bite into the soft flesh at her hips as I follow the movement of her body. My cock throbs, completely jealous of my face, but his turn is coming...literally.

"Wes...I'm so close. I can't believe..." Her words drift off in the night, replaced by a sharp keening cry that strokes my aching dick and a second later she's tumbling into a clitoral climax and releasing on my face. I tighten my hold on her hips and center her over my mouth. I put my tongue inside her, to give her something to clench onto and the room closes in on me as her flavor explodes on my tongue.

Fuck, how can she taste so goddamn good? I don't know but I want more, every fucking inch of this woman. I want my cock in her mouth, in her sweet pussy, between her luscious tits, fucking and claiming all of her. I know we don't have a future and I don't even care how insane that sounds right now, but I'm fucking lost in her.

I let her ride out the waves and once she's done, I flip her over. I study her face, her half-closed eyes, and my heart thumps double time. I touch her cheek, and with her liquid release wetting my face, I press my lips to hers. She moans and slides her hands around my back.

"I need to be inside you," I say.

Her lids open, and she swallows. "If it's what you want," she teases.

I go still. "Is it what you want, Charlie?"

Her eyes open wider, and while I don't want her thinking too hard, don't want reality to invade upon this fantasy, I desperately need to hear it.

"It's everything I want."

My throat tightens as need and want claw their way to the surface, and I ignore the drumming beat behind my eyes warning I might be opening myself up too much here.

"Condom," I say. Her eyes go wide, but I quickly address her concern. "I have one, don't worry."

I reach over the bed to grab my shorts and fish out a condom. I go back onto my heels between her spread legs, wide open and waiting for me. Jesus. I can't seem to take my eyes off her hot pussy, the way her release glistens on her soft folds. My stupid fingers, so anxious and needy, fumble with the foil and she takes it from me.

She finds the tear and opens it, and questioning eyes meet mine.

"I don't know, babe. If you touch me, I might explode."

"If you come, you come. We have all night, Wes," she whispers, and my heart twists into knots. Is she serious? She wants this as much as I do, and she's not upset that I might shoot off and blow it. Other women...let's just say, they wanted no rookie mistakes from the boy known as the Rookie. My face twists, and I grind my teeth to keep it together and she smiles at me, aware how close I am to losing it as she sheathes me.

Her touch is so soft, so gentle, I force myself to think about other things, like the game, the early morning practices, the cold rink.

She falls back onto the bed, and takes her gorgeous breasts into her hands. I can't take my eyes off her as she widens her legs in invitation. "What was that you said about needing to be inside me?"

My cock throbs, and I lightly brush her damp sex. "So pretty," I murmur and fall over her, shifting to position my cock at her sweet opening.

"Wes," she murmurs, and I inch back to see her face. "I want to feel you dripping out of me tomorrow."

"Holy fuck, Charlie."

"When I feel it, I'm going to remember this right here." She writhes beneath me, her hot cunt brushing against my crown. "I'm going to remember how good you make me feel."

"You don't have to hang on to this memory, Charlie." Why then am I keeping her shorts? "I'm going to fuck you so many times this weekend, I'm going to be dripping out of you for weeks."

A whimper of want catches in her throat. "God, I hope the cows never come home," she murmurs with a small laugh as she puts her legs around me, and I power into her. She gasps as her soft body opens up to accept every inch of me, and I keep driving until I hit her cervix, which brings on another low moan of pleasure from her. Her hot heat squeezes me tight, and I move against her.

Her hands slide around my back, and she drags my skin with her nails, marring my flesh. I love it. I want the scars on my back. I want the reminder. I inch out, meet her gaze, and hold it as I groan and slide back in.

"Wes, that is so good," she cries and bites against my shoulder. She's right, it is good. Honestly, her body fits with mine so well, it makes sex that much better than it's ever been before.

Her knees squeeze my sides, and she cups my face, and brings my lips to hers. Our tongues tangle in a flash of need, and her sweet little moans stroke my balls until they're tight, ready to explode. I strive to hang on as her muscles milk my orgasm, and I fuck her harder, nice long smooth strokes to take her body to where it needs to go again. I glance at her and her eyes roll back in her head. I push my pelvis against her clit, grind it with each downward thrust, and my name spills from her tongue as she releases around me in a rush of heat. Incredible.

I love seeing her like this, so open, so ridiculously aroused that she doesn't have a care in the world and I sense that's not really like her. No, this girl carries a lot on her shoulders in the run of a day and I'm glad I could help her escape reality, even if it's just for this weekend.

What if I want more?

That thought hits like a puck to the teeth, and I push it back. More with her is out of the question, right?

I bury my face in her neck and breathe in her sweet smell as my entire body throbs with pleasure.

"Yes," she murmurs, and my dick thickens more, and I cant my hips forward and release high inside her. "I feel you. So good," she murmurs, her voice low, so sated, my chest puffs, the caveman in me pounding his chest in pride. Ridiculous, I know, but to give her mind-blowing sex does something crazy to me.

I fall over her, crush her body against mine as I find her lips again. I kiss her softly, a light brush of our lips. "It's a good thing this dome isn't made of real snow," I whisper, and she starts laughing, a light, airy sound like for the first time in a long time the weight of the world is off her shoulders.

"You're right," she says. "We would have melted it and created an igloo tsunami."

"I can see the headlines now: two locals drown in a puddle of incredible sex." She goes a bit quiet, and I brush her hair from her face. "Hey, what is it?"

She stifles a yawn. "You're not really a local, not anymore."

"Yeah, but you know what I mean."

She nods, but her brow is furrowed. "It really was great sex, Wes."

"For me too, babe." I inch out of her, and she yawns again. I grin, "I'm sorry I kept you up so late."

"No, you're not," she says with a tired chuckle that curls around me and hugs tight. I hug her to me, unable to get close enough. "You're just being polite."

I laugh. "Okay, maybe you're right."

I throw my legs over the side of the bed, and remove the condom. I wrap it in tissue and toss it into the garbage can. "Be right back." I take a trip to the bathroom and warm a washcloth to clean her up. I come back out, and her eyes are sliding shut, but she's working hard to keep them open.

"Hey sleepy girl."

"I'm awake," she murmurs. I position myself on the foot of the bed, and spread her legs. She forces her eyes open and moans when I press the hot cloth to her sweet pussy. I wipe her gently, and she writhes against me. Christ, I fucking love the way she reacts to my touch.

I finish cleaning her, toss the cloth aside, and crawl in with her, tugging the covers up to keep her warm.

"You can't do that, Wes," she says, her voice groggy. She rolls into me, throws one leg and one arm over me as she presses her face to my chest.

"Can't do what?" I ask, my heart pounding a bit faster, worried I did something she didn't like.

"You can't arouse me all over again, and not do anything about it."

My heart settles as I chuckle. "I plan to do something about it, just later."

A long beat of silence and I'm pretty sure she's asleep when she murmurs, "I want more."

I glance down at her, my arm around her head, her face squished on my chest. "You...want more?" I ask. Have her thoughts been going down the same path as mine? The truth is that we barely know each other, yet we've known of each other forever. We had one day of adventure, and one night of incredible sex, but goddammit, something is happening between us. Or maybe it's just happening with me. Rider once said to me, when it comes to the right girl, you just know. But that's crazy. I once thought that about Breton and look where that led.

She's not Breton.

Maybe not, and maybe there's something in the fresh ocean air messing with my brain. I'm a guy who swore he'd never get involved with a hometown girl searching for a way out, right? Now suddenly I want to be the guy to take her where she wants to go. What if I do, though? What if I ask the girl looking for bigger and better to go to Seattle with me? Will she bail once she realizes I'm simply a small-town farmer who's good at hockey? Or am I letting old fears mess with my head and my heart?

"Yeah, this weekend, before we go home and back to reality, I want more," she clarifies.

"Right, and believe me, you're getting more. But first you're going to close your eyes and get a few minutes' sleep. After you have a power nap, I plan to mess with you again." She moans and snuggles in deeper. I tighten the blankets around us, and just before I drift off, she mumbles something in her sleep.

Did she just tell me not to mess with her heart?

I'm honestly not sure, and maybe I should be more worried that she's going to mess with mine.

12

CHARLIE

I turn to my side, and muscles I didn't know existed groan in protest. What the heck is going on with my body? I work hard every day, lifting and lugging lobster bins, not to mention controlling a big vessel in the open Atlantic waters. My muscles shouldn't be sore. I move again, and realize it's not my biceps hurting. Nope, it's muscles deep between my legs that haven't been used in a long time that are fighting back in the most glorious ways.

With a smile on my face as delicious memories of last night bombard me, and warm every inch of my well-used body, I peel my eyes open. My God, the sex was incredible, the best I've ever had and there's no denying I want more. I search my brain. Did I tell Wes that last night? Did I tell him I wanted more while we were living in some fantasy world on Brier Island? Honestly, I'm not sure. He fucked me so thoroughly, it was all I could do to keep my eyes open after that first round, and when I woke up in the middle of the night, I woke him up by climbing on his body and rubbing myself all over him. My smile widens at the memory of his face when his eyes opened to find me on top of him.

I reach across the bed, wanting to go for round three, or four. Five? I laugh quietly. He's turning me into a sex maniac, and I've totally lost track of how many times he was inside me, and yes, I have to admit, I am a little worried that after him any other man will fail to live up. My fingers come up empty and an uneasy feeling moves through me. I turn to find the bed vacant and cold, and disappointment floods me.

I briefly pinch my eyes shut to pull myself together. *This is sex, Charlie.* The fact that he's not in my bed this morning—or rather his bed—is no big deal. We slept together, but it doesn't mean we have to snuggle when the sun rises. Speaking of the rising sun, I glance at the clock and curse under my breath. Goddammit, I should have been up an hour ago, getting breakfast ready, and preparing for today's adventure. Some host I'm turning out to be.

I kick my blankets off, and go searching for my pajama shorts from last night. I move things around and when I get a chill, I tug on Wes' T-shirt draped over the chair, the one he'd given me on the boat to wear. When my search for my shorts comes up empty, I hurry up the ladder and snatch up a clean pair of panties and shorts and make a fast trip to the bathroom to brush my teeth and get cleaned up.

I take in the dark smudges under my eyes, compliments of a late night. After a quick shower, and praying that my guests aren't all waiting around for me, I dress and exit the bathroom. In need of coffee, I go straight to the kitchenette to make a carafe, and go completely still when I find it's already brewing. Wes made the coffee? I chuckle. Of course, he did. He has it in his head that this weekend is all about him doing for me, and well...I secretly like it. I know, I know, I'm a strong, independent woman, but maybe I'm also a girl who likes to put herself in the hands of a take-charge, capable man who wants to lighten my load.

Cripes, last night he put my needs first, pleasuring me like it was his job, and I didn't hate it. Nope, not one little bit. I'm not sure I even knew what I liked or needed until he pushed me to tell him. Mom always said never to rely on a man, and I get it. We have to be able to take care of ourselves, but maybe it's okay if we let someone take care of us once in a while, too—at least in the bedroom. Lord knows I've been taking care of that task for far too long.

Why wasn't he in bed when you woke, Charlie?

As that question dances around in my head again, all kinds of answers come to mind. I'm pretty sure I told him I wanted more, but maybe he's a one and done kind of guy. Get what he wants and moves on. I need to be okay with that, even though there's a niggling in my brain that tells me that thought is way off base, that he's not a guy to hit it and quit it. There's another part of my brain, however, telling me, despite what Jules said, that he's been with a lot of different women, that he has a revolving door, that he might still be in love with his ex.

Stop!!

I take a deep breath to still my thoughts. I have to stop overthinking this. Wes and I had sex. Period. Nothing else. I told him one weekend of fantasy, and under no circumstances am I going to fall for him. I can't—won't—be that stupid.

I glance at the counter, and the second I do, my heart does a little somersault, and I fear I could be *that stupid* when I find a note on the counter. I pick it up, run my finger over Wes' handwritten words, my breath fluttering a little in my chest.

Get some rest, babe. Gone for a run, and I'll take care of breakfast when I get back.

Could the guy be any sweeter?

Hey Charlie, did you sign up for the girls' team by mistake?

I push that memory to the back of my brain. He's obviously not that mean boy anymore. My stomach flies high as I pour a big mug of coffee and add a splash of milk. Hushed voices from outside reach my ears, and I walk to the door and peek out and find Wes and Rider coming back from a run. They're talking quietly, about what I don't know, but judging by the intense look on their faces, I think it might be something serious.

I open the door, and as a cool ocean breeze washes over me, two heads jerk my way. Oh, God, did I interrupt? My chest tightens and I begin to back away, when Wes' lips curl up in a ravenous smile. A hard quake goes through me. He walks up to me, all hot and sweaty from his run, and it's insane how sexy he looks.

I call out to Rider. "Give me five minutes and I'll get right at cooking us breakfast."

Wes snorts, and calls over his shoulder. "Give us thirty minutes, or make it yourself."

Rider gives a knowing laugh and heads toward his dome. "Why did you say that?" I ask, and try to look past him again, to tell Rider breakfast will be shortly when Wes starts backing me up and the door slams shut behind us. He reaches behind himself and sets the lock. As he shuts the world out and us in, a quiver goes down my spine.

There's an intensity about him, an animal chasing its prey, as heat radiates from his body. His scent reaches my nose—all musky and full of testosterone—as his body bumps mine. God, I like it. "Wes? Is everything okay?"

"No."

My breath stalls in my lungs. What is going on with him. Is he regretting last night? No, that can't be it. He wouldn't have left a note, being so damn sweet. But maybe on his run he thought things through and decided once was enough with me. Did I disappoint him? I mean, I'm not all that experienced but I'm sure he was having a good time.

"What...?"

"We need thirty minutes, because one of two things are about to happen." The urgency in his voice sets my pulse racing. His gaze moves over me, and his jaw clenches when I take the hem of the shirt I'm wearing—his shirt—and ball it in my fists. "I need you now, this very second, so you either join me in that shower—although I doubt that the two of us will fit without some creative maneuvering—because baby, I need to fuck you. Or I bend you over this table and take you even though I'm all sweaty. Choice is yours, Charlie. Make it fast."

His breath is coming harder now, and I don't think it was because of his run. His hand slides around me and he tugs me to him, anchoring me against his raging erection. I gulp, shocked at the heat and want simmering in his eyes—thrilled at the way he wants me.

My sex grows wet, dampening my panties. "That's what the guest wants?"

He growls. "Yes."

Never having been so bold or brazen behind closed doors— this man really brings out a different side of me—I push away from him and his eyes narrow in on me, like an animal ready to take chase, but I'm not about to run. No, I'm about to give myself over to him, in ways that I probably shouldn't—in ways that could prove to be dangerous later on.

I turn and wiggle my hips as I shimmy my shorts to my knees, leaving my panties in place, my mind recalling how he loved dipping into my pajama shorts last night. Okay, and maybe I liked that too. Who knew?

"I like you all hot and sweaty, farm boy," I say, and love his responding growl and how it curls around me.

"Fuck me."

I glance at him over my shoulder and my sex clenches as I take in the way his body is trembling—for me.

"No, Wes. Fuck me."

He takes a breath and exhales slowly as he closes the small gap between us, and my nipples pucker in anticipation of his touch. Not disappointing me, he slides his hands around my waist, dipping under my shirt, and sliding up to cup my aching breasts. I whimper.

"I was gone too long, wasn't I?"

"Yes," I murmur and push my breasts into his big warm hands. He breathes against my neck, his breath scorching my skin.

"Poor baby, woke up so needy for my cock and I wasn't here to give it to you. Did you have to touch yourself?"

Playing along, I whimper. "It wouldn't have been the same. Only your cock would do, Wes."

He curses under his breath, and my chest swells. God, I love what I do to him—what he does to me. I don't know if he's like this with every girl, and right now I don't care. I'm staying in this fantasy for as long as possible.

"I'm so sorry," he whispers against my neck, my hair fluttering with his harsh breath. "You were sleeping so soundly, I thought I could get a run in, but it's hard to do with a raging fucking hard on."

I chuckle, but it's tortured and needy. He plays with my hard nipples before sliding one hand lower. Deft fingers toy with the elastic on my panties, and I moan for more.

"You need this?" he asks.

"I need you."

He rewards me by sliding a hand inside my panties, the rough pad of his finger grazing my aching clit. More tortured curses reach my ears when his fingers slick over my wet sex.

"I think you should put your hard cock inside me. I can't have my guests running around the island sporting a hard on."

"Not good for business?" he teases.

"Probably not, especially if you walk out of this dome without one."

"Not going to happen. As long as you're around, I'm going to be hard, babe."

A thrill goes through me. "I have to see what I can do to keep that under control. I can't have any potential guests thinking I provide anything other than camping services."

He slips a finger into me and I moan. "No, this is only for me?"

"Yes, only for you."

"Fuck yeah," he says in a voice so deep and possessive as he strokes my G-spot, I nearly come around his finger. "Only for me."

I move, rock my hips as he finger fucks me right here at the kitchen table. One hand goes to my back and he runs his fingers down my spine, pressing hard enough to send shivers through me. I whimper and circle my hips, wanting him deeper...wanting his cock.

"Cock, please..."

"We'll get there, baby."

He fucks me with his finger, pulling out only to slide in again, and I'm so damn wet and slippery, it seems to be driving him wild. He's grunting and panting, and just when I think I'm going to come, he slowly inches out of me. I whimper my protest and he chuckles against my throat.

His breath travels down my back as he sinks to his knees. I go wild as he takes his time adjusting my panties, fitting them nicely around my ass. He lightly rubs my ass cheeks. "So pretty. Have you ever been fucked here?" he asks, and my resulting gasp answers his question. "Maybe you'd like that before we leave this island." He tugs my panties down in the back, to expose my ass, and he presses slow kisses to my cheeks as he massages with his big hands, tugging to open me and I damn near lose my mind as pleasure centers between my legs.

He pulls my panties back up, another prolonged foreplay session meant to drive me delirious. My panties bunch as he tugs them high, making a thong, and with each, hard upward pull, he stimulates my swollen clit. This man knows all the tricks and I love it.

"Rub yourself against your panties, Charlie. Show me how you get off."

"Holy God, Wes," I say, and thrust back and forth against my panties, as he holds them tight against my pussy and ass. "That feels so good."

"Let see how this feels." He tugs my panties down, and I'm about to widen my legs to give him full access, when he squeezes them together, puts his hand on my back and bends me forward until my nipples are pressed against the kitchen table.

The rustling of clothes reach my ears as he tugs off his sweaty running clothes, and I moan when he taps my ass with his cock. He rubs it all over me, and gently parts my cheeks with it. Is he going to fuck me like this? Equal measures of excitement and fear grip my stomach. I did say I wanted to do everything with him, but do I dare let him take me like this?

"Relax babe, right now my cock wants inside your hot pussy, but my tongue is getting there first."

I claw at the table, and try to open my legs again but he restrains me and that, weirdly, comes with its own pleasure. I whimper, and he buries his face in my pussy from behind, his tongue so hot against my wet flesh, it's almost too much. He licks me, pushes his tongue into me, and my God, I really wish I could watch.

He takes his time playing with me, alternating between his tongue and finger, toying with me like I'm a plaything. But each touch brings me closer and closer to release, because yeah, he damn well knows what he's doing.

"So tight," he murmurs and slides two fingers into me. The fit is incredibly tight in the position he has me, and I'm not even sure he'll be able to get his cock in. I can't wait for him to try. He repositions, and puts his palm over my clit, applying pressure as his fingers work my hot sex from behind.

My breathing grows harsh, and I scratch at the table, sure I'm marring it. "Wes..."

He stills his thick fingers inside me. "Take what you need from my fingers, fuck them for me. Show me what you like and let me watch you get off."

I begin moving like a girl on a mission. Riding him hard and fast as he keeps pressure to my clit, and within seconds the room closes in on me as light flashes before my eyes and I tumble into a powerful orgasm. I pant, gasp, and pound at the table, and tears, happy tears, prick my eyes.

"I love making you come," he murmurs, and stays on his knees as I continue to clench around him. My juice drips down his hand, and coats my inner thighs, and the next thing I know he's spreading my legs and sliding his tongue over my flesh.

"Fuck, you taste good." He finishes lapping at me and stands. I'm about to lift myself from the table but one big hand holds me down hard, and my heart leaps. I never knew I like being restrained like this. Foil reaches my ears and a stupid, ridiculous idea crashes through me. I bite down on my cheek. Don't say it, Charlie. Don't freaking say it.

"I'm on the pill," I blurt out.

Dammit, I said it.

He goes completely still behind me. "Charlie?"

I angle my head, take in the intensity on his face. His jaw is so tight he's going to snap something.

"Never mind," I say quickly. I turn back around and press my cheek to the cool table. "I shouldn't have said that."

I remain still as he takes a big breath, lets it out slowly, and repeats it three more times. "Do you want me to fuck you without protection?"

Way to not let it go, Wes.

"I shouldn't have said that. It's stupid and irresponsible." I turn my face the other way, not wanting him to see the flush of embarrassment.

"For the record, I've never had sex without a condom."

"Right, which is why I shouldn't have said that. You don't take chances. I get it."

"We wouldn't be taking a chance. You're on the pill."

My brain races then slow. His words twist with the arousal inside me, and I can't quite figure out if he wants to, or doesn't want to.

"Wes?"

"I want to fuck you without a condom, Charlie," he answers, his words firm, confident, definitive as he slides a finger into me, and I gasp. "I want to feel your flesh on my cock, the same way I feel it on my finger."

"I...I want that too."

"I'm clean. I promise," he says and when I hear the quiver in his voice, I look back at him and when I do, I spot vulnerability. It wraps around my heart and makes me want him even more. I have no idea why I like him like this, unsure, almost a little afraid. I guess it reminds me he's more than a cocky NHL player. That at the heart of the matter, he's a small-town farmer with compassion and integrity.

Don't fall for him Charlie.

I swallow down the unwanted emotions rising in me. "I'm clean too."

"I know."

"I want to feel your cum drip out of me all day, Wes. When I do, I'll bite my lip to let you know."

"Fuck." He tosses the condom away and rubs the wet tip of his cock all over my ass before aligning it with my opening. "Are you comfortable in this position?" he asks quietly, his voice so strained and needy, I quake with want.

"Yes, please, Wes. Please put your cock in me," I plead, my voice a low needy whisper.

He jerks his hips forward and slides into me. I'm so wet he easily glides all the way in, despite the way my legs are clamped together. Everything about this feels deliciously dirty as he begins to pump, long hard strokes, but what I like the best is the raw, animalistic grunting sounds he's making.

I move with him, rocking to meet each hard thrust, and once again I start clawing at the table as pleasure builds, my nipples roughly rubbing against the hard wood.

His big hand splays on my back, and the warmth spreads through every cell in my body. I whimper quietly, loving everything about this.

We move in sync, our moans of pleasure merging in the dome, not a care about us, other than pleasure. He reaches around my body, and his finger sluices over my wet clit, and I cry out louder. I'm sure our neighbors can hear, I'm sure I scared all the seals back into the water, but I can't seem to help myself.

"Yeah, just like that," he encourages me as my muscles clench around him. I take a fast breath and when I let it go, my body lets go with it, my hot juices coating his pistoning cock. "Fuck, you are scorching."

He thickens inside me, stretches me in glorious ways. "Fill me with your cum, Wes."

As soon as the words leave my mouth, his hands go to my hips for leverage, and he drives all the way inside me, releasing as he hits my cervix, which, catching me by surprise, brings on another full orgasm for me.

"Ohmigod, yes!" I whimper and rotate my hips as he spurts his seed inside me, his warmth traveling through my body, and awakening far too many things inside me.

I pant against the table, and he falls over my back. Soft fingers brush my hair from my face and neck, and he peppers me with open-mouthed kisses that leave my skin wet.

A moment later, he lifts himself, pulling me up with him. He turns me, picks me up and sets my bare ass on the table. Without words, he slides his hand around my neck and presses soft lips to mine for a kiss so tender and gentle, a kiss so steeped in need and openness, my heart does a somersault.

He inches back, his eyes darker now, sated, as they move over my face. A grin slowly shapes his mouth. "I kind of just ravished you."

"I kind of just let you."

"I'd say I'm sorry, going at you like a damn caveman, all sweaty like this. I'm just not sure I am."

I run my finger down his glistening chest. "Didn't you know that was the best part for me?"

He laughs, slides his hand around my neck again and kisses me. "I do now." He taps my ass. "Why don't you get a shower first, and I follow behind."

I crinkle my nose. "I guess it is kind of small for two. I must remember that if I build more of these domes. I guess I didn't have shower sex on the brain. We'll miss out on that."

"Or not."

Before I can ask what he means, he slaps me again. "Now go, and leave it running, I'll come in behind you."

I grin. "That sounds interesting, and dirty."

He laughs as I slip away, and jump into the shower. The water feels glorious against my flesh, and I let it drip down over my sex. But I don't linger. Wes is waiting his turn and I have guests next door.

I wash quickly, and step out to find Wes standing there, his cock semi-hard. "You were watching this whole time?"

"It's like you don't know me at all," he teases.

"I don't really know you, Wes."

His brow furrows for a fast second, and I can't help but wonder what I said to upset him. He steps up to me, drops a soft kiss onto my mouth. "I'll be fast. I know you're anxious to get to the others." My heart skips a beat at his thoughtfulness. His fingers brush my cheek and as I stare at him, a new kind of intimacy, closeness, a comfort that I've not felt with anyone in my entire freaking life cocoons me.

Oh boy, I could be in so much trouble here.

13

WES

"Why does this bacon taste so good?" Charlie asks and stares at the thick, crispy pieces between her fingers like it might hold all the answers to the universe.

Jules takes a sip of her coffee and exhales, contentment all over her as she sets it down. "It's because someone else cooked it." She flicks a finger at me as I hover over the small outdoor stove and frying pan. "It's always better when someone else cooks."

I grin, loving how much the girls have bonded. It's clear Charlie needs a friend, and I bet anything all the players' wives would love her as much as we all do. The wives come from different backgrounds, with different interests, yet are very inclusive. I have no doubt they'd take Charlie under their wings in a heartbeat. I smile as I consider it, my mind's eye visualizing them all at Watauga Beach, sipping wine and sharing stories over a bonfire. The lake and campfires are totally Charlie's jam.

Wait, what the hell am I thinking? When would they ever cross paths?

"Well then," Charlie says and points to me with a thick slice of bacon. "Wes, you can do all the cooking from now on."

"I don't mind. I actually enjoy it," I say, as I scramble the eggs and pour them into the pan.

"Knitting and cooking," Jules says and nudges Rider. "You could learn a thing or two."

"Hey, I cook," he says, feigning indignation. "But no, I am not learning to knit." He takes a bite of toast, not about to entertain the thoughts of learning. The guys have playfully been razzing me about my knitting skills since they found out, yet they've all been asking me to knit them something else after Mom supplied the team with toques.

"I wouldn't mind learning," Charlie says. "I could use some good warm clothes, especially if I have to move to Toronto."

Have to? She says that like she doesn't want to. Sometimes she really confuses me. One minute it seems like she's anxious to get out of here—heck, the first time she jumped on her boat and I asked where she was going she said anywhere but here—then other times she seems anxious to stay. When I see her in her element, I know rural Nova Scotia is where she belongs. Does she know where she belongs?

Jules' jaw drops open, incredulous, as her hands still, her toast inches from her mouth. "Why on earth would you move to Toronto and leave all this behind?"

"She applied for jobs there," Rider says, and suddenly, as if he said something he wasn't supposed to, his gaze jerks to mine. I turn to Charlie, to find her frowning at me.

Shit. I give her an apologetic shrug, and hope I didn't over-step by sharing something personal with Rider. It's just that on our run, I brought it up—yeah, I really like thinking and talking about Charlie—and I'm still not sure why I told him about the job offers. I guess maybe the idea doesn't sit well with me, and that could be for purely selfish reasons, like if I come back to my hometown, I like the idea of her being here. But he was a good sounding board and offered up some advice, that I'm currently running around my brain, but will probably never follow up on.

"Sorry, it just sort of came up when we were out running earlier. I hope you don't mind."

"It's okay. I don't mind. I guess you guys must have ran out of things to talk about. Me moving to Toronto is hardly newsworthy."

She's wrong...it's newsworthy to me.

"Why on earth would you go to Toronto?" Jules says, her eyes narrowed like she can't wrap her brain around it. She widens her arms and looks around. "You love what you do here. This is where you belong. Everyone knows that."

Charlie smiles, but it's forced and doesn't reach her pretty eyes. "This..." She glances around with awe and wonderment in her eyes as she takes in the ocean, the birds flying overhead and the creative, cozy campsite she made. "It's a side gig for the family business during the off season, and I have a management degree to put to use." She looks at her plate and picks at her toast when she adds, "I applied to a couple firms in Toronto. It's the right thing to do."

"When will you hear?" Jules asks.

Her brow furrows. "It's possible they emailed already, but I'll wait and check when we get back tomorrow."

She's nervous to check, that's pretty clear. Is it because she's afraid she didn't get a job, or is she afraid she did?

She tosses another piece of bacon into her mouth, lifts her head and plasters on a smile as she redirects. "Jules, do you like sea glass?"

"I love sea glass."

Rider throws his arm around his wife and once again, as I see the love they have for each other, jealousy tugs at me. Rider smiles at Jules. "She loves finding old things and making them new again. It's a hobby for her, and she's good at it."

"That's what she tried to do with Rider," I say, deadpan. "But she failed. He's still an old man."

"Asshole," Rider snorts. "We can't all be baby rookies like you."

"Baby rookie. I like that," Charlie says with a light laugh.

I point the spatula at her. "Careful there, Charlie." I slap the spatula against my palm. "You're younger than me by a few years."

Heat crawls up my neck when she glances at the spatula, like she has other ideas for it, and holy fuck, when she bites her lip, a private message to me, my cock jumps. "Only in age, not in maturity."

"You're probably right," I say and laugh.

She turns to Jules. "When the tide is out, we can go under the wharf, and find the best sea glass. I have a few pieces I made into jewelry." She shrugs. "I thought about selling some pieces in the shop, or at the weekend market."

I shake my head, not at all surprised. She is a born entrepreneur, with such great ideas and management skills. Any firm would be lucky to have her.

You'd be lucky to have her.

"I would love to see your pieces," Jules says.

"Yeah?"

"For sure. Would you be willing to sell a few? I've been trying to figure out what to bring back for my sisters and my girl-friends." A smile lights up her face. "Oh, Charlie, you would love all the wives of the players," Jules says, like she read my earlier thoughts and is going one step further with them. "Did you know Cole Callaghan's wife Nina is a New York times bestselling author? Maybe we can hit up a bookstore if we get into the city again. And Zander's wife Sam is a speech pathologist." She flops her hand out toward Rider. "Of course, you have to meet Kane, Rider's brother, and we've been trying to get him and my closest friend Lindsay to tie the knot forever." She rolls her eyes like it's been a huge chore. "Oh, Jonah's wife Quinn runs her own daycare in Boston, but the guys all have cottages at Watauga Beach. You'll love her. And—"

"Slow down, love," Rider says, giving her a loving hug. "She's not going to remember all those names."

Jules nods. "You're right. Anyway, I'll introduce you when you come to Seattle. Everyone is going to love you." She turns an eye to me. "We've been trying to talk Wes into getting a place on the beach, but we haven't been able to get him to bite yet. I heard from Fallon, that's Jamie's wife, that a new place went on the market." She points at me. "You'd better grab it before it sells."

"They're overtaking the entire lake. I think it could be a cult." I wink at Charlie. "Resistance is futile."

It doesn't pull a laugh from Charlie like I hoped, because yes, I like when she's happy. Instead, she sits there and blinks at all the information coming at her. "I probably won't be going to Seattle anytime soon."

"Oh well you never know," Jules says with a wave, like she doesn't believe that. "But you're invited to come stay with us anytime you'd like. Isn't that right, Rider?" She doesn't give Rider a chance to answer. "Or you could stay with baby Rookie." She grins at me. "He has a big place with lots of spare rooms. No matter where you decide to stay, I'd love to show you around my state." She holds a finger out and adds more as she starts listing off all the fun things to do in Seattle. "At Pike's market, there's this gum wall."

Charlie makes the same face Jules and Rider made when we told them about the beaver tails. "A gum wall?"

"Yeah, a gazillion pieces of gum stuck to it. I even put a glob there."

"That sounds...disgusting. Wait, how can you say Canadians are weird, when you have a gum wall?"

We all laugh, and I finish cooking the eggs and divvy them up. I finally sit to join in on the breakfast and Charlie pours me a big cup of coffee from the Thermos. I toss her a thankful smile, as I picture her touring Seattle. The four of us going out to dinner, and showing her all the places I think she'll love. Like I said, we haven't known each other long, but I've got a pretty good idea on what she'd like to see.

I toss a slice of bacon into my mouth and moan. "I don't think it's the cook, I think it's the bacon that tastes good," I point out.

Charlie looks pleased with herself. "I get it from a local butcher."

"Is this Canadian bacon?" Rider asks.

"In Canada, we just call it bacon," Charlie and I say at the exact same time, and then we laugh. I turn to her and we share a secret smile. I definitely think we're more alike than we realize and maybe she does see the farmer beneath the jersey, and maybe, just maybe, she likes that guy. I know I like the girl who wears rubber boots and overalls. A lot. Too much, probably.

"I don't know what it is about this place that makes me so hungry," Jules says as she forks egg into her mouth. She moans with pleasure as she chews and lifts her face to the breeze washing over us.

"Fresh ocean air," Charlie explains. "And wait until after our hike. You'll be ravenous."

"It's a good thing I'm only here for a week, otherwise I'd be the size of a whale. Then I'd be the one you'd be taking pictures of from the side of the boat."

Rider kisses her forehead. "You're beautiful no matter what."

"I'm a sure thing, babe," she says, playfully and nudges him. "No need to sweet talk me. Leave the sweet talking to Brody."

Charlie's eyes go wide. "Brody Tucker?"

"You know him?" I ask quickly, my voice suddenly deeper, possessive, thick with jealousy. Shit.

"I don't know him personally, but I do love him. He's my favorite defensive player. He made some great plays last season."

Jules grins at her. "He's single. If you come to Seattle, I can introduce the two of you."

My gut squeezes. If Jules is trying to lure the green-eyed monster lurking in the depths of my gut to the surface, she's succeeding. I chew my food harder, trying to dispel the image of Charlie with Brody, or any other guy for that matter. Fuck, I don't like that one little bit. But Christ, she's not mine. She can slide between the sheets with any guy she likes, and Brody isn't a bad guy. He's actually a great guy, and they'd probably have a great life together.

Fuck that, shit.

"You okay, Wes?" Jules asks, her voice light and easy, but it's the knowing grin on her face that gives her away. She's pushing my buttons because she thinks Charlie and I make a cute couple. I glare at her. I love Jules, I really do but Charlie and I can't have a future. Her life is here, soon to be in Toronto, and she told me this was just a fantasy weekend.

But I fucking like her. A lot.

"Yeah, just too busy eating to talk," I fib. I take a big sip of coffee and Charlie bites her lip as she refills my mug, and my mind goes back to when I had her bent over the table, filling her with my cum. Fuck me twice.

I go quiet and eat while Charlie and Jules talk about Nina's romance books, and the careers of the other women in our group. Charlie listens, fascinated, and once I finish scoffing my food, I start to gather up the plates.

"Leave them for us," Jules says. "I can't be useless all weekend." She glances at Rider. "Let's stack them for later. I'm anxious to go explore."

We stack the dishes in a bin and ten minutes later, we're all in the Jeep, with Charlie driving us to Pond Cove where we'll begin our hike. I take in the gorgeous scenery again as she drives, and Jules has her phone out to take a video.

"I can't wait to take Sophie here when she's big enough," Rider says.

"Yeah, she'll love this. Ohmigod, look at all the seals," Jules shrieks.

I gesture with a nod to the hill Charlie and I picnicked on. "We can go to the hill to get a better look."

"I am so glad we came here." I look over my shoulder to see Jules' huge smile. "What other things do you suggest we do when we're in town, Charlie?"

She puckers her lips in thought. "Next weekend is Digby Days. It's the town's big scallop festival."

"Right, I forgot about that," I say. "Are you away here doing tours on the weekend?"

She shakes her head. "No, I booked it off. My sister will be doing the tour." Charlie looks a bit sheepish when she says, "I'm signed up for the scallop shucking contest on Friday afternoon. The parade and most of the events are on Saturday, and of course fireworks both Friday and Saturday night."

I grin at her. "Scallop shucking? Are you kidding me?"

She lifts her chin. "I don't plan to relinquish my trophy any time soon."

I laugh. "You won last year?"

She blows on her knuckles and buffs them. "Uh, yeah."

"I can't wait to see you win this year," I say and give her a wink, totally impressed.

She crinkles her nose. "You don't have to watch. You'll probably be bored to death."

"Are you kidding me? I wouldn't miss you winning the title again for the world."

"I like your confidence in me."

"Charlie, you can do anything you put your mind to. I have no doubt."

She smiles and glances at Jules in the rearview mirror. "The festival starts Friday and runs until Sunday afternoon. Lots of people come from all over, and many who moved away come back home for it." I nod in agreement. Last year I never made it back. I was too busy setting up my life in Seattle. "You picked a good week to be here if you're into scallops and parades and fireworks."

"We're into all that stuff," Rider says.

"Don't forget I want to get back to the city," Jules says. "I want to try that restaurant we walked by last time."

"Which one?" Charlie asks.

"The Bicycle Thief, that fancy-looking place on the water with seats overlooking the harbor. I really want to get dressed up and enjoy a little fine dining in the city. Maybe we can do that Friday night after Charlie wins her shucking contest. That way we don't miss the parade Saturday, and we're up first thing to leave early Sunday."

Charlie nods. "It's such a great restaurant, Jules." I'm about to ask her to come along on a double date when she speaks. "During the festival there's a demonstration for scallop shucking on Saturday if you guys are interested. I'll be volunteering."

"I'm game for anything," Jules says, practically bouncing in her seat.

Charlie turns into the cove and parks. Jules jumps from the back seat to get a better look at the beach and seals and Rider follows her out.

I grin and give Charlie's leg a squeeze, thanking her for giving my friends such a nice adventure, and reminding me of the festival. "Come to dinner with us Friday night," I blurt out.

Her smile is forced. "You don't need me tagging along. You want some quiet time with your friends, don't you?"

"I want you tagging along."

She frowns. "I might have to work. Can I get back to you on that?"

I nod, but unease works its way through my body. Does she not like that restaurant? Or maybe getting dressed up isn't her thing. Maybe she doesn't have fancy clothes. Hell, she can go in her rubber boots for all I care.

"Ready?" she asks with a smile.

I nod and a few minutes later, we all have our backpacks on, and Charlie leads the way along the pathways, telling us how they're privately owned on Nature Conservancy of Canada land. She definitely knows a lot about a lot of things. Heck, I'm just a farmer who is good at hockey.

We walk for a long time along the windy pathway, the ocean breeze keeping us cool. Charlie comes to an abrupt stop and since I'm behind her, I bang into her. "Sorry," I say and slide my hand around her waist. Her entire body reacts, and my cock notices.

She turns and her cheeks are pink and I'm not entirely sure it's from the hike. She puts her fingers to her lips, and points. She crouches and we all follow her down. "That's Whipple Point," she explains. "It's a bird nesting area."

As birds take flight, Jules' face lights up and Charlie identifies all the different birds as they go overhead. "There are over one hundred and seventy species."

"I wish I had binoculars," Jules says just as Charlie unzips her backpack, reaches in and produces a pair. She hands them to Jules and for the next twenty minutes or so, we all take turns with them.

Charlie stands and brushes grass from her knees. "Follow me." We hike a bit longer, and then we come to a big grassy clearing.

"Um...is that a sheep?" Jules asks and Charlie and I turn to find her pointing at a fluffy sheep. Jules looks totally perplexed. "How did a sheep get on this island?"

"That's a South Down Babydoll." Charlie grins as she explains. "Have you heard of hooking?"

"Hooking?" I glance around. "Like...Hooking? As in prostitutes?"

"Ohmigod, Wes," Charlie says and whacks me. "Hooking, like in sheep wool hooking?" She glances at Jules and rolls her eyes. "Like I said, I'm older by maturity. Now come on, I want to introduce you to Victoria. She's going to give you a hands-on experience with the process."

I grin at Charlie, and like the ass I am, I put my mouth near her ear and tease, "When I get you back to the dome, I'm going to give you your very own hands-on experience."

She bites her lip and I damn near come in my shorts.

14

CHARLIE

The bell over the door rings and I glance up, half expecting Wes to come sauntering in. We've been back from Brier Island for four days now, and not a day has gone by that I haven't seen him, or hung out in some way. He's always popping in, making excuses as to why he's on the docks, but I think in my gut—and hope in my heart—it's because he wants to see me. Because he enjoys my company as much as I enjoy his. Who knew, huh? Who knew the infamous NHL player and the lobster girl would hit it off so well? Then again, he's really just a farm boy at heart, isn't he?

The truth is, I've gotten in deep with the farm boy, deeper than I should have allowed myself, because when he leaves for Seattle, I'm afraid I'll be going to Toronto with a hole in my chest and he'll be on a plane with my heart in his hand. We haven't spent a lot of time together, but we did spend quality time together, enough for me to realize just how amazing he is, and I have to admit, back in the day, despite the names he called me those few weeks during that hockey season, I always had a thing for Wes Hatfield.

A group of tourists come in and disappointment settles in my stomach. It's late afternoon and he's usually by long before now. My sister Jane comes from the backroom, and we ring in our customers. When the last person leaves through the door, I pull my phone from my back pocket and check my messages for the hundredth time. No matter how many times I read the messages from the two firms I interviewed at, they're still the same. It's been a few days now since I found out both firms want me, and both are awaiting a response.

As I tuck my phone back into my pocket, the sudden, desperate urge to divulge the information to Wes grips me hard. I'm not sure why I urgently need to tell him. Heck, I've been sitting on the news since we came back from Brier Island. I haven't even told my family, and I'm not sure why, since I know they're all waiting to hear, too. I tug my hat off and shake out my hair.

"Do you think you could close up for the day?" I ask my sister, as I remove my yellow gloves and drop them into an empty gray lobster bin.

Eyes that match mine twinkle. "Oh, off to see a hot hockey player?" she asks.

I roll my eyes at her and resist the urge to tell her he's so much more than that. "I'm actually going to see Jules. I want to talk to her about the festival tomorrow."

"Yeah, sure."

I step out from behind the counter, my stupid heart beating a little faster as I try to walk, and not run, to the door.

"I'll see you later."

"Say hello to Wes for me," Jane calls out.

"I will."

Shit.

Her laughter follows me out the door, and I guess the whole town now knows we've been hanging out, and of course, Breton thinks we're a couple and still isn't happy about it. She scowls at me every time I see her. But she doesn't need to get her panties in a twist, because there is a part of me that's worried Wes is still doing all this to make her jealous for reasons I don't want to think about.

I jump into my car and head toward the Hatfield farm. I wave to a few people out for a stroll and check my face in the mirror. I pinch my cheeks to give myself a bit of color and consider changing out of my work coveralls, but why bother? He's seen me in them before, and I'm not going to change who I am for anyone, right? Not that Wes is asking me too.

I take the twists and turns in the backroad and creep into his driveway, but his car is nowhere to be found. I'm about to back up when Mrs. Hatfield comes from the old farmhouse. She waves at me, and I park my car and climb out, the warm afternoon air falling over me.

"Mrs. Hatfield," I say. "How are you?"

"How many times have I told you to call me June? You and your three sisters, always with the Mrs. Hatfield."

I just laugh at that. "You've met my mother, right?"

Now she laughs. We were never allowed to address our elders as anything other than their proper titles, and I can't get out of the habit, even though I'm an adult now.

"Are you looking for Wes?"

I glance around, take in the tree branches swaying in the warm breeze as fresh floral scents fill my nostrils. "Yes, I guess I must have missed him."

"Nope, Rider and Jules went sightseeing, and Wes is helping on the hill." She turns to point, and I follow her gaze through the massive orchard. "He's fixing a fence back there. Why don't you head on over and say hello?"

I crinkle my nose and consider it. "I don't want to bother him if he's working."

"No bother at all." She waves one hand, like she's shooing away a fly. "I was just about to bring him water." She holds up a Thermos. "You'd be doing me a favor if you brought it to him."

"Oh, sure. Not a problem."

She hands me the bottle, and I head toward the hill. I check out all the buds on the trees as I make the long trek up the hill, following the sound of a hammer hitting a nail as it echoes in the vast space. In the distance, a cow mooing reaches my ears and I grin as it reminds me of our intimate time on the island. As those thoughts go through my head, my body warms and it has nothing to do with the late afternoon sun.

I'm breathless when I reach the top, and I can barely speak when I spot a shirtless Wes standing there in nothing but jeans and work boots driving nails into a wooden fence.

Holy farm boy hotness.

I gasp, and sputter and try to fill my lungs, and the ridiculous sounds have him turning my way. I bend forward, and with the Thermos tucked under my arm, I brace my hands on my knees and take gulping breaths.

"Hill," I manage to get out, but I'm pretty fit so I think my body is reacting to the gorgeous sight before me. A smile splits his kissable lips, and he drops the hammer.

Before I even realize what's happening, he hurries to me, scoops me up and sets my ass on the fence. He inches my legs open, stands between them and twists the lid off the Thermos.

"It's a big hill," he says. "Take a few breaths and then drink."

I do as he says, and he tips the cold water to my lips. I take a big drink, and when I'm done, he does the same. He tightens the lid and drops it to the ground. I inhale, glance around, and try to sound normal when I speak. "The valley is beautiful from up here."

"I know," he says, as I try not to think about the way he's spreading my legs, and getting himself a little closer to the needy spot between my legs. You know what else I'm trying not to think about? How sweaty he is, and how much I like it.

"Jules and Rider are gone out?" I ask, even though Mrs. Hatfield already told me they were.

"I think they needed some quiet time, and it gave me a chance to help Mom and Dad with things around here."

"You like working on the farm?"

He nods, and for a second I get the sense that my presence here has really thrown him off. Did he not want me to see him working up here, or something?

"I don't mind helping out. It's good work, lots of time to think."

My gaze narrows in on him, and I note the seriousness about him. "Do you have a lot to think about?"

The truth is thinking is all I've been doing since we returned from Brier Island. Thinking and fantasizing and wondering what if...where Wes is concerned.

"Yeah," I do. His eyes narrow for a second, and then he smiles. "What are you doing here?"

What *am* I doing here? Jeez, I don't even remember. It's awfully hard to think straight when my body is aching for his touch again. He reaches up and lightly caresses my hair away from my face, his big rough hand is so gentle against my skin. "I...I...was thinking."

He angles his head. "About?"

"What we did on Brier Island. Maybe we could..."

God, what am I doing?

His grin is broad and wicked, and his hands clench my thighs. "You want to mess around, Charlie?"

No, I want to get serious.

Shit.

"If you do," I say for lack of anything else, and hope I'm not making a fool of myself.

He holds his hand up. "You see these calluses."

I lightly touch his thick, hard calluses, and his face twists like he's in total agony. "Yeah."

"They're not from the hammer."

Heat rockets through me as understanding dawns. "They're from the hose?"

I bite back a grin as he stares at me for one long second, then he bursts out laughing. His arms slide around me and he pulls me onto his waist. I wrap my legs around him as he carries me along the upper edge of the property.

I slide my hands around his shoulders and lock them together. "Where are you taking me?"

"Down there," he says, and off in the distance I see a pond. "I'm all hot and sweaty."

I run my fingers through his hair. "Did you forget that I like you this way? But you know, it does look refreshing."

He grins and starts walking down a winding path, with me in his arms. "I don't have a bathing suit."

"Don't need one." He reaches the pond, and I expect him to set me down and strip off when he starts walking right into the cool water.

I shriek. "We're in our clothes."

"They'll dry." He sinks down, bringing me to my neck and the cool water seeps into my coveralls.

"That is so nice." I unwrap my body from his and push off. Without taking his eyes off me, he reaches down, and I can only guess he's undressing. I stand, and slide my overall strap from my shoulders, and shimmy out of the wet material. Before I tug my T-shirt, bra and panties off, I glance around. "I'm not going to flash anyone, am I?"

"Just the beaver if it comes back, and of course me." He wags his eyebrows playfully. "Now you have three seconds to get naked before I start ripping your clothes." I grin, loving the urgency about him. He moves to the bank, sits down and takes off his pants and shorts.

"What if someone comes?" I ask.

"That's the plan, Charlie."

I chuckle at his joke, despite the shiver that just went down my spine, and I go to work on stripping and he disappears under the water, coming up right in front of me. Big hands grip my panties and he disappears again as he tugs them down my legs, and a laugh bubbles up in my throat as I lift one leg and then the other. My God, he is so much fun, so spontaneous. Easy and relaxed to be around. I love being with him.

I love him.

Shit.

He tosses my panties to the side, and I throw my bra away without a care in the world, other than feeling this man inside me again. He pulls me against him, and his erection presses against my leg as he sinks down to take my breasts into his mouth. I throw my head back, never so reckless in my life, and give myself over to him.

He moans and the vibrations go through my body. I grip his hair, hold his head to me, and my body burns from the inside out, despite the cool water. One hand slides between my legs, and he eases a finger into me. He finger fucks me for a few minutes, until I'm so close to coming, and while my vibrator didn't give me calluses on my hands, it was Wes on my mind when I used it these last few nights. This is so much better. This is...everything.

"God, yes," I murmur, not wanting to be too loud, or sound too alarming. I'm not interested in putting on a show for anyone other than the man with his finger inside me. He pulls it out, and cups my breasts.

"I have totally not spent enough time here," he murmurs and slides his tongue around my nipple. He squeezes my breasts together, and his cock throbs against my legs. "One of these days I'm going to fuck you right here."

I gulp as he worships my body and glances up at me, a promise of things to come in his eyes. "Yes please…"

He grins, and starts backing up, dragging me with him. He reaches the embankment, and hauls himself out, until he's sitting on the edge his feet still in the water. "I want you on top, baby. I want you to ride my cock so I can see your face when you come all over me."

I put my legs around him and shimmy up. His hands grip my waist and he holds me over his erect cock. I wiggle as he pulls me down and a cry lodges in my throat as he slides in so deep, it brings on a full body quake.

"You good?" he asks, his voice soft and gentle, deeply inti-mate, as big hands brush my hair from my cheeks, and his eyes move over my face, a careful check in.

"Better than good." I roll my hips, and his cock hits all the right spots as I move.

"Yeah, baby. Just like that." I lift myself up and fall back onto his cock. "I've wanted to do this all week," he admits. "All I wanted was back inside you."

I grip his shoulders and bring my lips to his. He kisses me, devours my mouth, as I ride him, his gorgeous cock sliding in and out easily as I grow wetter.

"Babe, so fucking good."

"I know," I agree, and he slides a hand between our bodies to apply the perfect amount of pressure to my clit, knowing exactly how and what I like. I do love a fast learner. I straighten, and rub my breasts on his face as I bounce on his cock, and he grows impossibly thicker inside me.

I ride him hard, and toss my head back as our bodies slap together. Heat barrels through me, and somewhere in the distance a bird takes flight, no doubt frightened by our mingling moans. Keeping one hand on my clit, he slides the other up my back and holds me. I move, restless, needy as I chase an orgasm. I rock, ride him and I cry out as pleasure centers on my core.

My lids fall shut, every cell in my body tingling in bliss. "Wes," I murmur, unable to find the words to describe how good this is with him.

"I know, babe. I know," he responds, just as lost in me as I am in him. I force my eyes open, and note the way he's watching me, and just like that, my body lets go of everything except pleasure. Heat pours from me, and he grunts his approval as it drips down his pistoning cock.

His jaw clenches as I move my hips, wanting every inch of him inside as I clench around his thickness.

He swallows, and a tortured noise crawls out of his throat. "I'm...there."

"Come inside me, Wes. I want to feel you drip out of me again."

"Fuck, yeah." His hand tightens on the back of my neck and he holds me down as he shoots his seed high inside my body. I close my eyes and savor the sensations, loving how good I can make him feel. He grunts a couple more times and guides my mouth to his when he finally stops spurting.

We press our lips tighter and because my orgasm drained the last of my energy, we both just cling and breathe together, our lips lightly brushing. He puts both arms around me and holds me to him so tightly, it squeezes the air from my lungs. I lay my head on his shoulder and breathe in his skin as we both slowly come back. His cock grows soft inside me, and he lifts me up, and I nibble my lips as a few droplets spill out of me.

"Charlie?" he asks, breaking the quiet.

I sit on his lap, and breathe, "Yeah."

He brushes my wet hair back and cups my face. "Feel free to visit me on the farm any time you want." I grin at him and as my body comes down from the high, my smile falls. "Hey what's wrong?" The worry in his eyes, the genuine concern tugs at my heart.

"I remembered why I came here."

"It wasn't for this?" he asks and points a finger back and forth between the two of us, his brow raised in curiosity. "Checking to see if I finally became a better kisser?"

I chuckle, but my insides are a mess. "You're a great kisser and you damn well know it."

"What's going on?" he asks, humor gone from his voice.

"I wanted to tell you. I got an offer from both those firms where I interviewed."

He goes deadly quiet, his eyes narrowed in on me, like he's trying to find the right words, and my God, I really want him to find the right words—even though I'm not entirely sure what they are. My throat tightens, and I hold my breath as I wait for him to say something in response.

He exhales, and nods his head, like he's coming to terms with something. "Congratulations and I'm not surprised. You're good at everything you do."

My stomach sinks, and I resist the urge to jump from his lap and run until I can't run anymore. Honestly, what did I expect him to say? *Oh, Charlie, don't go. You know right here is where you're supposed to be—here with me.*

I force a smile. "Thanks."

Why, oh why did I let myself fall for a guy who will be leaving here soon? This is just sex, nothing more. Plus, I think he's still hung up on his ex, so why would he try to talk me out of Toronto, talk me out of moving away from my beloved town and give up my summer tours on Brier Island—my very own Disneyland, where I'm the happiest. But this isn't a Disney movie and happily ever after doesn't exist in this world. If it did, Wes would have taken a deeper interest in me, and understood who I was much like I figured out he was a simple farm boy beneath the jersey. Heck, the first thing out of Jules' mouth when she heard about Toronto was that I belonged here. Maybe I'm the only one feeling the pull between us, and maybe this was a good reminder of what's real and what isn't.

15

—

WES

I don't want her to go to Toronto. Hell, the only place I want her to go is with me, to Seattle. Not that I think she should leave here, but she's definitely determined, and I guess I can understand why.

Rider slaps my back as Jules walks ahead, her high heels clicking as she browses the tables lining the shore. It's Friday afternoon, and Digby Days have started, which means all the local vendors are out selling their products and Jules is having the time of her life. But we're all dressed to head to the city for dinner after the festivities. Jules is in a form-fitting cocktail dress and Rider and I are in khaki pants and collared shirts.

He casts me a worried glance. "Have you thought any more about what we talked about on the island?"

I nod. "I put a few calls in to the team manager and I'm waiting to hear back. I just don't want to overstep, you know." I suck in air, and worry about that. Charlie is an independent woman, but before I say anything to her, I want to make sure my ducks are all in a row.

Rider fixes his ball cap. "You also don't want her going to Toronto and having a life that doesn't involve you, right?"

I nod, and adjust my ball cap as well when out-of-towners start pointing at Rider and me.

"Don't worry," Rider says. "You'll get used to all the attention."

"I don't think I ever will."

He grins as a bunch of people come over to us, and we spend the next twenty minutes or so greeting fans and taking pictures. Jules finally arrives with a bag full of jams, jewelry and other local crafts.

"Come on guys." She checks her watch. "It's time for Charlie's shucking contest. I don't want to miss it."

The streets are busy as we walk further along the shore, and I glance up to see my cousin Lester. I love the guy, he's my cousin, but he's also a huge pain in the ass, not to mention loud and obnoxious. I don't even want to introduce him to Charlie because he's such a womanizer. Lester goes off to the beer tent, and we continue on, and as I watch him go, I don't watch where I'm going, and I smack right into Breton.

"Whoa," I say and wrap my arms around her before she topples backward and lands on her ass. "Sorry. I didn't see you there."

She pushes her hair back and smiles at me. "Just the three of you? Where's the fourth wheel?" She glances over her shoulder and laughs. "Oh, right, she's busy shucking scallops. That's attractive."

I gesture with a nod for Rider and Jules to head on over to Charlie's event while I deal with Breton, and they walk off. Breton smooths her hand down her light summer dress, the top two buttons undone to showcase her ample cleavage, but I don't look. I don't want to.

She blinks at me, and pushes her breasts into my chest. "Do you want to get together later at the beer tent? Maybe we can play some pool, for old times' sake."

"Can't. Busy." I glance over Breton's head, and make eye contact with Charlie, and that's when I realize I still have my arms around Breton. I pull back, and Breton pouts.

"Just a short game." She winks. "Winner takes all."

"I'm with Charlie now."

Her eyes go venomous, but she quickly blinks it away. "I'm sorry for what happened between us, Wes. I made a big mistake dating Sam, but you and I both still have feelings for each other."

She's right about one thing. I do have feelings for her, and they're based on contempt. "The past is the past, Breton. None of it matters now."

"Maybe it does matter."

I have no idea why she's being coy, but I play along. "Why?"

"The past might not stay in the past, and you should probably be aware of that."

"What are you talking about."

"Sam is back for the festival." She jerks her thumb over her shoulder and sticks her hip out in a seductive move that once drove me wild. "He spent an awfully long time chatting it up with Charlie. I'm not sure I ever heard her laugh so hard. I was almost convinced she wasn't playing for the other team."

"She's not," I say through clenched teeth, as old insecurities come back to haunt me, but I don't want to show that in front of Breton.

"Then I guess she must totally be into Sam, considering the way she was giggling at whatever it was he was saying. Pathetic really."

"They're friends." I take a few deep breaths as the world tilts on its axis.

"Sam and Charlotte, that has a nice ring to it." She laughs. "Did you know he calls her Charlotte?"

My jaw begins to ache from all the clenching. "Yes."

"Wes," she says quietly. "You know we were meant to be together." She toys with the collar on my shirt. "Can't you forgive me?" She blinks thick lashes, and makes a pouty face. "I know this whole thing with Charlie is to make me jealous. You could have picked a prettier girl, but still, I get what you're doing. I'm sure Charlie figured it out by now, too. But I'm a sure thing, Wes. She's not the girl for you. We could make a good life together."

"Did you say something to her, about making you jealous?"

She rolls her eyes. "No, but it's just so obvious. She's so not your type."

"It's over between us, Breton. It has been for a long time now. If you'll excuse me." I walk past her, and her huff reaches my ears. Christ, is it possible that Charlie thinks I'm using her to get Breton back? That's crazy, right? The things we've shared, the honesty and openness. We're building something here, right? Or was Charlie just having a bit of fun with the NHL player?

Fuck.

I head toward the long table set up for the shucking contest and Charlie's head lifts, her lashes rising and falling slowly as she meets my gaze, and I smile at her. "Everything okay?" she asks.

"Yeah, uh...Breton. I banged..." Her eyes widen and I shake my head. "Not like that. I wasn't looking and banged into her."

She nods and turns her attention to the judge, a crusty old fisherman with skin made of leather, as he picks up a microphone and speaks.

Jules claps her hands. "You got this, Charlie."

Charlie casts her a quick smile just as my phone rings. Shit. I grab it from my pocket, and caller display informs me it's the team's manager. As much as I want to watch Charlie shuck and win, I have to take this call. I glance at her and mouth the words sorry as I point to my phone. She smiles but it's forced.

I slide my finger across the screen, put the phone to my ear, and close my hand over the other to block out the noise. "Hey Mike, thanks for getting back to me."

I spend the next ten minutes chatting, and there's a new lightness—hopefulness—in my gut when I hang up. I hurry back to my friends, and exchange a glance with Rider. He arches a brow in question, and I give a nod.

"How is she doing?" I ask.

"I think she's winning, but I lost count."

I let the excitement wash through my body, anxious to talk to Charlie later tonight and praying she'll come with us to dinner. I arranged a special gift for her just for the occasion. As a new kind of urgency wells up inside me, I root her on, and she is so damn impressive. Shucking scallops like she's a pro, and well really, she is. I take in her competition. Mostly burly men three times her age, and one elderly woman who I recognize as a cook from the Lobster Shack.

"Two minutes left," the judge calls out, and one man yelps, having cut himself. First aid runs to him, and gets him bandaged up, but he's out of the competition. Now I'm worried for Charlie. Her fingers are moving so fast, and I didn't even realize how dangerous this could be.

The judge begins a countdown and we all do it with him. He blows a horn to signal the end and everyone raises their hands. I grin as I glance at Charlie, who has scallop juice on her face and in her hair. The judge starts counting the scallops in their bowls.

She's not into NFL superstar Sam Gilmore, right?

With two job offers in Toronto, she has a way out of here and doesn't need Sam. Not that I think she's that kind of girl, she's not. Funny thing is, for the very first time in my life, I want to be a girl's ticket out of Digby, Nova Scotia. What's not funny is, she doesn't want to go. Sure, there is a part of her that needs to go, but her heart and soul are here in Nova Scotia, and I might just have the perfect solution.

Jesus, don't let me fuck this up.

"Hey dude, there you are," Les says and slaps me on the back. "Big-ass superstar, don't even make time for your cousin, anymore."

"Just been busy," I say, and smile at him. "Les, meet my friends Rider and Jules."

"Rider Lewis. I'm a fan, man." He zeroes in on Jules and swipes his long hair from his forehead. "Jules, a gorgeous name for a gorgeous woman."

"Cool it, cousin." I give him a shove before Rider does. "Jules is Rider's wife."

He laughs and winks at Rider. "Sorry, dude."

"And the winner is Charlie Baxter," the judge says and holds Charlie's arm in the air. She smiles from ear to ear, but it falters when she sees me standing next to my cousin.

"Is that little Charlie Baxter all grown up?" Les asks, and gives a low slow whistle. "Wow, I think I need to talk to her."

"No, you don't."

He grins at me, and rips my ballcap from my head. "What, are you into her or something?"

"Or something," I say and snatch my hat back before he can put it on.

"You've got to be kidding me?" He laughs like this is all a big joke. "Little miss coveralls is not your style, dude." He glances at Breton as she walks by and eyes me, and a horrible, uneasy feeling mushrooms in my gut.

Before I can answer, Charlie comes walking over, a shiny trophy in her hand. "That's really something to be proud of, *Charlie*," Breton calls out, emphasizing her name.

Charlie's footsteps still for a second, and her smile falters. Fucking Breton. She has no right to make Charlie feel bad about her accomplishments or her name.

"You did great," I say, and hold my hand out to her. She comes closer, and I put my arm around her. My cousin shakes his head, clearly confused. What he doesn't realize is Charlie is ten—one hundred—times the woman Breton will ever be. She's kind and generous, and open and giving, and would never purposely hurt anyone, or use anyone to get ahead.

"Little Charlie Baxter," Les says and my skin crawls as he gives her a once over. I'm about to stand in between them, but Charlie can hold her own.

I glance at Charlie and wave my hand toward Les. "This is my cousin, Les."

"Wow, you two look a lot alike," she says.

"I thought you didn't know each other," I say. "But Les here seems to know you."

"I don't know him," she says quickly, and for the first time, I sense something is off, that she might not be telling me the truth.

"Come on, *Charlotte*," Les says. "How could you ever forget the guy who nicknamed you Charlie." He snorts. "Got everyone else to do it too, until it stuck."

Her jaw drops open and her gaze goes from Les, to me, back to Les. "That was you?" She blinks, her mouth opening and closing, incredulously. "I don't get it. How was that you? The guys were all calling you Wes."

As the pieces of the puzzle begin to click into place, I shake my head. "Jesus. Les was here for a few weeks while I was away at camp. I'm guessing you thought he was me, and they were calling him Les, not Wes. He's Lester. after his grandfather. I'm Weston. after mine. I can see why you made the mistake."

She nods her eyes wide as she glares at Les. "You're the guy who ridiculed me, asked me if I signed up for the wrong team because I hadn't developed boobs yet."

He grins, like he's proud of it. "I see things have changed." His gaze drops to her chest, and fury rips through me. I'm about to stand between them, punch my cousin in the mouth, when Charlie puts her hand on me to stop me.

"What you did was mean. You know what's worse. All this time I thought it was Wes." She turns to me. "I avoided you for years after that. Whenever you came into the Lobster Pound, I hid out back. I'm sorry I ever thought you were like that. After running into you this time, and getting to know you, none of it made sense." She turns to Jules and she's smiling and nodding in understanding. "I told Jules about it, and even she couldn't believe it was true. I'm sorry, Wes. I should have known better."

"That's why you hated me." I snort. "I get it. I would have hated me too."

"So, do you want to punch him, or do you want me to?" she says deadpan, but I catch the gleam in her eye.

"I think you should."

"Hey wait, what?" Les says, putting his hands up and inching back. "If you think I'm letting a girl punch me and I'm not going to punch back, you're wrong."

"See. Asshole," I say as I look at Charlie. "Told you." I turn to Les. "You won't have a chance to punch back. Charlie's just won a shucking contest that takes skill and strength. She carries bins of lobster twice the size of her, and can outperform any one of these fishermen on a fishing boat. But you have to the count of three to decide what you want to do." I pause, so proud of Charlie, so happy she knows I'd never treat her with disrespect, and then begin counting. "One...two..."

Les takes off running and I throw my arm around Charlie, and we all laugh.

She shakes her head. "All this time I thought it was you."

"Yet you still..." I wink at her. "You know."

"Well, you are a famous NHL player, and I needed that notch on my bedpost," she teases.

We all laugh, but a weird sensation grips my stomach. That's not how she really sees me, right? God, Breton must have really gotten under my skin for me to be questioning everything.

"Can we head to the city now?" Jules asks. "I made a reservation at the restaurant for seven."

Charlie checks the time on her phone, and cringes when she sees scallop membrane on her arm and coveralls. "Right, you guys had better get going, and you all look amazing by the way."

Jules frowns. "Aren't you coming?"

"You guys don't want me tagging along. You're not here much longer." She swipes her hand through her hair and something that looks like a sliver of scallop shell falls out. "Besides, I'm kind of a mess."

"We have time for you to shower. Please come. I made reservations for four people," Jules begs, and big blue eyes glance up at me.

"Please..."

Her lids briefly fall shut in thought and when they open again, I spot worry when she says, "Okay, I need a few minutes to get ready."

"Rider and Jules can browse the vendors for a little longer, and I'll drive you."

"I can..." she exhales and grins at me. "Fine." She eyes me as we make our way to my car. "Do you always get your own way?"

"So far with you I have," I tease. "And I hope that doesn't change before the end of the night."

"What's that supposed to mean?"

"You'll see."

"Wes! What are you up to?"

CHARLIE

I keep my eye on Wes as he drives, and he can whistle innocently, but that doesn't mean he's not up to something. I'm not sure what he has up his sleeve, but I know whatever it is, it'll be a blast. Everything I do with him is fun and I can't believe it was his cousin who started the nickname. All these years, I hid from Wes when I could have been...

Could have been what?

I certainly wasn't Wes's type back in the day, and I'm not his type now, but then again, maybe I am. I'm the one in the car with him, about to go to a fancy dinner. Maybe his tastes have changed and I wasn't just the first and only girl standing at Jack's Fish Shack, ready and able to help him out of a situation. Maybe I was the girl he wanted—chose—to help him out, for personal reasons. I'm pretty sure he likes what he's sees when he looks at me, and that he's not bothered by the scallop juice all over my face and clothes. Still though, there's a part of me that worries he's too good to be true. A laugh bubbles in my throat, because yeah, he's definitely too good to be true.

"Something funny?"

I turn to see him smirking at me. "Just thinking about you."

He reaches across the car and gives my hand a squeeze. "I'm funny."

"Sometimes." Honestly, I probably shouldn't be going to a nice, intimate dinner with him. I debated on whether to go or not since Jules first brought it up. It's just that I'm already in so deep, that spending more time with him isn't wise, because I can't see a future between us. But here I am anyway, agreeing to everything this man wants—what I want, too.

His phone rings and he pulls it from his pocket. He frowns, hits decline and turns it so I can't see who's calling. He shoves it under his leg.

A strange uneasy feeling creeps along my spine. "Aren't you going to get that?"

He stares straight ahead, his brow furrowed. "It's nothing." From the look on his face, I'd say it was everything. He casts me a fast glance. "I'll call back while you're getting ready."

I nod, and clamp my mouth shut before I ask if it's the same caller from earlier, the same caller who pulled him away from my shucking event, when he vowed he wouldn't miss for the world. Clearly someone on the other end of that phone must be more important than the world. It's not my business, so I keep quiet. We reach my house, and I open the door. He doesn't budge, so I turn to him.

"Are you coming in?"

He picks his phone up and shakes it. "You go ahead. I have a call to make."

I nod, slide from the vehicle, and shut the door. I take a breath, and work to ignore the unease careening through my blood, my intuition telling me something isn't right. I hurry up the stairs, drop my trophy into my room and head to the shower, quickly scrubbing the day from my skin. With a towel wrapped around me, I dart to my bedroom and come to a complete stop when I spot a gorgeous dress on my bed —which I hadn't noticed earlier. It's the same dress I saw in the shop window when I was on the waterfront with Wes and his friends. I pick it up to examine it, and check the size. A perfect fit. Jules said she thought this would look good on me. Did she...buy it for me? Why would she do that?

"So pretty."

I spin and find Mom standing there, her feet crossed as she leans against the doorjamb her arms folded across her chest. Her blue eyes twinkle as she studies my face.

I frown and take the plastic off the dress. "When did this come?"

"Earlier today."

"Who...who is it from?"

"It arrived by courier with only your name pinned to the plastic." Her brows lift. "You didn't order it?"

I rub the silky fabric between my fingers. "No."

Mom pushes off the doorframe and walks to my window. "Maybe the guy down there has something to do with it."

I follow her to the window and glance out to see Wes standing by his car, his phone pressed to his ear. What is going on with him?

"He and his friends asked me to join them in the city for dinner," I explain.

"And he bought you a dress." She turns and smiles at me. "How nice of him."

Is it, though? Is it nice, or is he worried that I'll wear coveralls to a fancy restaurant and embarrass him? As that worry burrows like a thirsty tick, I walk to my closet and flip through my clothes.

"You're not going to wear it?"

I give a non-committal shrug. "I don't know."

"It's very lovely, Charlotte."

I glance back over my shoulder, my body tight. I have to be reading this situation all wrong. Wes isn't trying to make me into something I'm not. This is just a nice gesture, and I can't let what happened to Mom cloud my relationship with Wes. Right?

My brain settles, and I come to a fast conclusion. "I'm going to wear it."

Mom nods. "It's going to look gorgeous on you. I have just the pair of shoes to go with it."

"Shoes, right. You mean I can't wear my rubbers?" I tease with a grin, getting a little more excited to go to the city, to spend a romantic evening with Wes and his friends.

"You could, obviously, and no doubt rock them, but I think heels would go better." Mom disappears, and I slip into the dress, and spin in front of the mirror. Once again, I feel like Cinderella, with all the birds chirping joyously around my head.

Mom gasps when she comes back. "You are simply gorgeous, Charlotte."

I smile. "You have to say that, you're my mother."

She laughs. "If you don't believe me, just wait until Wes sees you in this."

I like the idea of impressing Wes, of him taking this dress *off* me. "Mom...?"

"Yeah."

She sets the shoes down and I slip into them. Back in front of the mirror, I turn left and right to examine the flare in the dress. I really do love the way it fits my body. "Do you like Wes?"

"Of course, I do. He's a nice boy. He was always very sweet when he came to pick up the lobster shells, and his folks are lovely. They raised a good farm boy."

"A farm boy," I say under my breath. "He's a big NHL player now, though."

"Maybe, but you can take the boy out of the farm, but you can't take the farm out of the boy."

I nod in agreement, having said something similar myself not so long ago. "That's what happened to you, right? You went to the city, but at the heart of it all, you belonged here."

"That's right. I couldn't get the ocean or the lobster trolling out of my soul. The sea isn't in everyone's soul, though," she warns quietly.

"I know."

She steps up to me, and tucks my hair behind my ears. "You need experiences to discover who you really are and what you really want."

I smile and hug my mother. It's important to her that I go to Toronto, or somewhere, and experience other things in life. She doesn't believe that I know what I want just yet, but I do, and I don't want to disappoint her by not going out in life and experience new things, especially after she worked so hard to put me through college. I owe her that. I'm just not sure I'll be happy in Toronto. I'm also beginning to wonder if I'll be happy here once Wes leaves.

How did I get myself into such a mess?

"Now why don't you go see Wes's reaction when he sees you in this dress."

I laugh, a little bubble of joy welling up inside me. I negotiate the stairs carefully. I'm not used to heels and when I step outside, find Wes leaning against his car waiting for me, the look on his face sends a thrill straight to my heart.

"Thank you," I say and swing the hem of the dress. "It's beautiful."

"I saw you admiring it. I hope you don't mind that I ordered it for you."

"You didn't have to. I have dresses."

He smiles. "It's just you seemed so unsure those times I asked you to join us."

I resist the urge to tell him it's because the more time I spend with him, the more I'm falling for him. "I didn't want to intrude."

"Never." He steps around the vehicle and opens the door. "Jules helped me figure out your size."

"It's a perfect fit. Like it was made for me."

Like *he* was made for me.

He climbs in beside me, and I fold my hands on my lap as we make our way back to the shore to pick up Jules and Rider. They climb into the back seat and Jules squeals.

"I knew that would look amazing on you."

"It was quite the surprise," I say.

Jules laughs. "Sneaky Wes."

Could his private phone calls have something to do with the dress? Probably not, especially if it was delivered earlier, like Mom said. We pull onto the road, and I spot Breton near the beer tent, her fingers flying across her phone. Just then Wes' phone pings, and my throat tightens. Are they texting? Worry creeps through me as our earlier conversation about why he kissed me dances in my brain. Could this be about making her jealous and winning her back?

"You okay?" Wes asks, his brow furrowed as he gives my hand a squeeze.

"Yes, just tired. Shucking takes a lot out of you," I tease.

We all fall into easy conversation as we drive to the city, and Jules talks about how much she'll miss it here, but is looking forward to seeing it through her daughter's eyes when she's old enough. She once again invites me to Seattle, and I give a halfhearted answer. Wes remains quiet on the subject which makes me worry that he's not all that interested in me visiting.

He pulls into a parking spot at the restaurant and the sea breeze falls over us as we climb out of the car. The boardwalk is busy with tourists and locals alike and even though both Wes and Rider are dressed up, they put on their ballcaps and pull them low. We're seated at a lovely outdoor table, overlooking the Halifax Harbor, and the two guys remove their hats, which creates a lot of fanfare, but most fans walk by, stealing a picture, not wanting to disturb them when they're out for a meal.

We order wine and beer, and laugh and tell stories as we devour a ton of appetizers and pasta. It's a great night, one of the best nights of my life, in fact, and by the time our dishes are cleared and the dessert menus are handed out, I turn to Jules and shake my head as I pat my swollen stomach.

"What was that you said about being the size of a whale when you leave here?" Sadness invades my thoughts as I think about how our fun is coming to an end. I'm going to miss them. I'm going to miss Wes.

"But we're still having dessert, right?" Rider asks and pulls his wife in for a hug.

"Of course," she says. "Did you see this strawberry shortcake biscuit?"

I glance at Wes and groan, "I'm not sure I can do it."

"Split it with me?" he asks.

I nod, and for some strange reason, it seems oddly intimate—especially after everything we've done.

"Let's split one too," Jules says to Rider.

We put in our order and Jules stares out at the ocean. "I really can't wait to come back here."

"You're always welcome," I say.

She frowns. "But it won't be the same if you're not here."

My gaze goes to Wes, but he's checking something on his phone. What, does he have a hot date later? Soon our dessert comes, and as I dig into the fresh strawberries, I try not to think about the tightness in my chest, making breathing a little more difficult. Wes shifts restlessly beside me, and I turn to him.

"Everything okay?" I ask, aware of the new nervous energy about him as our meal comes to an end.

He smiles. "Yeah, I just need to talk to you about something later, okay?"

I nod and try to keep a smile on my face, even though there's a storm going on inside me. I have a bad feeling, and I'm not sure why. Or maybe I do.

After we finish our dessert and coffee, Wes insists on paying, and we all stroll the boardwalk, our bellies so full it's hard to walk. I notice the way Wes keeps looking at me, but I'm guessing he wants me alone before he tells me what's on his mind.

Off in the distance, I spot a guy around our age staring at Wes, and of course a lot of people are whispering and pointing. The man comes toward us, a huge smile on his face. Wes goes still.

"Owen?"

"Wes, I thought that was you." He throws his arms out and they hug. I glance at Jules and Rider and they shrug as lost as I am. Wes and Owen laugh, and pat each other on the back, that masculine way guys do.

Wes turns to us. "Owen and I were at hockey camp together many years ago."

"I'm so happy you made the NHL, bud," Owen says, and his eyes get big when he sees Rider. "Rider Lewis. Wow, so nice to meet you. I'm a huge fan." He shakes Rider's hand and glances at Jules.

"Jules, this is Owen. Owen, this is Jules, Rider's wife. They're visiting from Seattle." Wes explains and then puts his arm around my back. "This is Charlotte, she's from Nova Scotia. We both grew up in Digby."

Charlotte?

Did he just call me Charlotte, or is my hearing going?

"Nice to meet you, Charlotte," Owen says. "I'm here visiting with my wife and daughter." He glances around. "They're off getting ice cream, and I'd better go find them before mine melts."

The guys give another shake goodbye and promise to keep in touch, and we all head to the car. Once inside, I try to loosen the knot in my stomach—which has nothing to do with eating too much. Why didn't he introduce me as Charlie? Does he not like my name, or maybe he finds it too masculine, and Charlotte is more fitting for a girl in a dress? Is he changing me into what he wants? First the dress and now the name.

"You're awfully quiet," he says on the drive home.

I force a smile. "Just tired."

"Do you think we'll be back in time for the fireworks?" Rider asks.

Wes glances at him in the rearview mirror, and I take in his handsome profile, the smoothness in his shaved face. I resist the urge to touch him, as a part of me fears I'll never get to touch him again. "If I speed."

He steps on the gas and a yawn pulls at me. While I want to call it a night, I also don't. Wes wants to talk to me, and I want to hear what he has to say. I do worry, tonight might be his goodbye to me, but there is a part of me that hopes he's asking for more. I want that, even though a relationship seems impossible, with both of us going our separate ways. I don't see how a future could work, yet it's not stopping me from wanting one.

We finally make it back to town, and with the streets crowded, it takes time to find parking. The vendors are all packing up for the night and the beer garden is hopping as locals and visitors wait for the fireworks to begin.

Jules grabs my arm and gives a little tug. "Let's grab a drink."

"We'll get them," Rider says, and bends to give Jules a loving kiss on the forehead, and my heart misses a beat. I want what they have. "Why don't you girls try to find us a table."

I nod, and glance around. That's when I spot Sam Gilmore, a loud crowd around him. For a second I wonder if Breton might try to get him back, now that he's home. "That's Sam," I say to Jules. "Are you a football fan?"

She shakes her head. "Not really."

"Do you mind if I go say hello?" I'd spotted him earlier, before the shucking contest, but never had a chance to see how he's doing.

"Not at all." She waves me off. "I'll find us a table."

I head over to Sam and since he's taller than everyone around him, he spots me coming. He pushes from the crowd and comes my way, a wide smile on his handsome face. I smile up at him, so happy his dreams have come true.

"Charlotte," he says his arms out, a low whistle escaping his mouth when he sees my dress. "Since when did you get all fancied up for the fireworks?"

I laugh and hug him. "I was out to dinner with Wes Hatfield and Rider Lewis, and Rider's wife, Jules."

"No way, they're in town." He searches the crowd. "I have to say hello." He zeroes back in on me. "But first, how are you?"

We spend a few minutes talking, and I notice the sudden stiffness in his body, when he glances over my head, his gaze focused on something—or someone—in the distance.

"What's going on?"

I turn to find Breton all over Wes, as he stands there with two beers in his hand. But Wes isn't looking at Breton, he's staring at me.

"Are they back together?" Sam asks.

"I...don't think so."

"I always thought they were a good couple. Breton never did tell me why they broke up." He shakes his head. "Wait, you just said you were out to dinner with Wes." He waves his finger back and forth between the two of us. "Are you and him...a couple?"

"Um...no...yes...it's complicated."

"If looks could kill, I'd be dead, Charlotte. You better go see what's going on. I'll talk to you later, okay?"

He backs up, and I head toward Wes and Breton. Cripes, she's got her hands all over him, and he doesn't look very comfortable. Is it because he doesn't want her touching him, or he doesn't want me to see it? My heart beats faster, harder...erratic.

"Hey," I say, struggling to keep my voice normal when the sound has to pass over the lump in my throat.

Breton turns and glares at me. "What do you want?"

"Breton," Wes warns through clenched teeth. "Don't."

"Don't what?" She blinks at Wes. "Don't tell her that you succeeded in making me jealous, and yes, I do want to get back together."

My stomach squeezes tight, as fear circles my brain. "Wes?" I stand on shaky legs. "Is that true?"

Tell me it's not. Please tell me it's not.

"We need to talk," he says quickly.

Oh, God, it's true.

The room spins before me, and I stand here dazed, working to form a coherent sentence. "Um, okay?"

He takes a big, uneven breath. "Breton, can you excuse us please?"

Before she leaves she glares at me and says, "His slumming days are over, Charlie."

I try to get air as she walks away, try to keep my heart from crumbling. Wes' hand shakes as he passes me a beer. Mine shakes as I accept it, although there is no way I'll be able to swallow this, not with my throat so tight.

"Are you two getting back together?" I bluntly ask.

"What, no."

"The phone calls, and texts. That was Breton?"

"No, not at all."

"You weren't trying to make her jealous? When I asked about that, asked you if you were faking it with me to show her it was over, you said 'something like that.' It was about getting back together?"

"It's not like that."

I stand on wobbly legs and hold my own, even though my insides are a quivering mess. "Tell me what it is like."

"My team is hiring a part time manager," he begins quickly, like he can't get the words out fast enough. "I've been going back and forth with the head manager all day. I didn't want to say anything until I was sure, but he wants to interview you for the job. He's very impressed with all you've done. He told me if you're as good as I say you are, the job is yours. You'd be based out of Seattle, and..." I falter backward as understanding fully dawns, and his words fall off. "Are you okay?"

He reaches for me, but I step back, putting a measure of distance between us. If he touches me, I might very well shatter. I pinch my eyes shut. With everything coming at me so fast, it's hard to keep up. My brain races.

Wes wants me to move to Seattle?

My head drops, and tears pound behind my eyes as I stare at the pretty dress, eager to get out of it and back into my own clothes. I bite the inside of my cheek to fight a big ugly sob, and lift my head, doing my best not to fall apart in front of the man I've fallen in love with, the man who knows nothing about me.

"Charlotte?"

"Charlotte? What happened to Charlie?" I ask as I set my drink down on the nearest table before I drop it. "That name only suits me when I'm in coveralls, not when I'm dressed up, or at a fancy restaurant with you?"

A line forms in his forehead as he frowns, his panicked gaze racing over my face. "I thought—"

I grip the table, sure my knees are going to give out. "You thought you could change me into what you want. The dress, the name, the job. I'm not Breton. I'll never be Breton, or any of the other bunnies I've seen you photographed with." My God, how could I have been so wrong? How could I have thought he was a sweet farm boy, when he's really a player who wants me to fit into his lifestyle, all the while ignoring mine?

The line in his forehead deepens, and he backs up like I'd just slapped him. That's when I realize I'm causing a scene. I fold my arms over my stomach as it roils.

"I...I never said you were Breton, or any other girl."

"No, you just want me to be like them in every other way."

"Charlotte..." He tugs on his collar. "I mean...Charlie." His eyes briefly close, and they're full of bewilderment and agony when he opens them again. "Please. Can we just talk about this?"

"No, Wes. I believe you've said..." I glance at the dress again. "With and without words, all I need to hear."

His head hangs, his face tight. "I'm sorry."

"Sorry...you're sorry. That's all you have to say."

"I overstepped, I get it. I didn't mean..." His voice falls off as he fists his hair, his breaths coming faster.

Overstepped!

Trying to change me into his vision of a woman, yeah that's overstepping. "I thought..." I swallow against the stupid lump expanding in my throat. "I thought you knew who I was."

"I do know who you are, just like you know who I am."

"Actually, you don't know me at all, Wes." I fight to stay strong, to keep my voice even, but I'm breaking inside. No man has ever made me break before. *And why is that, Charlie?* Oh, because I've always kept myself closed off. With Wes, it was different. He dug a tunnel through my barriers, and I happily let him. "Just like I don't know who you are. I thought I did, but I was wrong." I shake my head and take another step back. My tight throat turns my next words into a garbled mess. "I made a mistake."

Sam jumps up as I back away on shaky legs, and I'm not sure what Wes is saying to me as I flee. The next thing I know Sam's arm is around me and he's guiding me out. Wes shouts something, but my rattled brain can't quite comprehend.

There's only one thing that I fully understand. Disney isn't real. Happily ever after doesn't exist, and I'm no Cinderella in need of a transformation before Prince Charming loves her. I want to be loved for exactly who I am—not who someone else wants me to be.

WES

What the ever-loving fuck just happened?

As I watch her walk off with Sam, his arm around her body, the same body I made love to numerous times, my heart thumps against my chest. No matter how many times I said it was just sex, I knew it wasn't. No, what we were doing wasn't sex at all. It was making love. At least it was on my part and honest to God, the pain I felt when Breton left me for Sam, walking away because I was a simple farm boy, is nothing compared to the pain I'm feeling now.

I take gulping breaths as voices reach my ears, everyone staring as I stand here, confused, barely able to fill my lungs as the vision of Charlie and Sam exit the tent and disappear into the crowd swims before my eyes. I try to make a move to run, to go after her, to claim her as mine, but I can't seem to make my legs work, can't handle her rejecting me twice in one night.

Fuck. Fuck. Fuck.

A big firm hand lands on my shoulder, and I turn to see Rider and Jules standing there, worry all over their faces. My throat hurts as I fight not to lose it, and cry all over my friend's shoulder.

"What's going on?" Rider asks, his gaze going from me, to the crowd, back to me. He moves his body, shifts to block me from curious eyes and phones, and people starts snapping pictures. Christ, this is probably going to be all over the news tomorrow and I fucking hate being in the public eye, and no one will get this story right. How could they? I don't even fucking know what happened myself. That won't stop them from spinning a goddamn tale, though. I just hope Charlie doesn't get dragged down. Sure, she just walked away with Sam, and left me standing here confused, gutted, broken-hearted, but that doesn't mean I want anything bad to happen to her.

"Charlie told Jules that guy was Sam," Rider says, pulling my thoughts back. "Sam as in Sam Gilmore...The guy who..."

He lets his words fall off, like he can't bring himself to finish the sentence, for fear of hurting me. I snort, my fingers curling at my sides and finish it for him. "Yes. That's Sam Gilmore. The one and only Sam, who Breton left me for back in high school." I stand there, unable to wrap my brain around the fact that Charlie just left with him. Why the fuck is history repeating itself? What the hell did I do in a past lifetime to deserve this?

"I don't understand," Jules says quietly as she shuffles a little closer, when people bang into her, trying to get close to over-hear our conversation.

"That makes two of us." I pinch the bridge of my nose, and struggle to fill my lungs as the room spins. I wobble slightly.

Rider puts his hand on my back, and gives me a nudge. "Let's get out of here."

I let him lead me outside, and if he didn't have a grip on my shirt, I'm sure I'd face plant, although I don't much care. I can't hurt any more than I already do. Fireworks light up the night sky when we get outside, and I glance around, searching for Charlie, but she's nowhere to be found. Maybe if I checked Sam's place, I'd find her.

"Fuck," I curse as Jules moves to the other side of me, the two flanking me and offering comfort, though I'm not sure anything can take the chill out of my bones, the pain from my heart.

Rider herds us to the quiet dock, away from prying eyes, and we walk the long length until we get to the end of it. I drop down, and let my legs dangle over the side. My friends position themselves on either side of me and mimic my position.

We sit quietly for a long time as fireworks crack around us. After what feels like an eternity, the fireworks eventually stop, the night sky going quiet again, and I take gulping breaths to calm my heart before I turn to my friends.

"I don't know what's going on."

Jules shifts beside me, like she's digging in and not leaving this wharf until we figure things out, and I make things right with Charlie. While I appreciate that, I'm not sure what I did wrong, or how to fix it.

"What were you guys talking about?" Jules asks, going in to nurse mode so she can make everything better again, although I'm not so sure she can.

"I told her about the job for the Seattle Shooters." I jerk my head to the right, toward my buddy. "Rider mentioned they were looking for a part time manager. I've been making calls all day. I thought she'd be perfect for it. I'd arranged a job interview. I was telling her about that. I was excited about it. I thought she would be too. It meant we could be...together."

"Oh," Jules says, her voice low and breathless.

"I overstepped." I lean forward, brace my elbows on my legs, and rest my chin in my hands as I glance out over the water, the sound of the waves crashing against the dock, cutting through the silence.

"I don't think she wants to leave here, Wes," Jules says quietly.

"I know."

"Then why did you..."

Her voice falls silent, and my mind races, going over the events of tonight, of the last week, of the first time I set eyes on Charlie at the rink when we were kids, when she impressed me with her hockey skills. Fuck, no one has ever impressed me quite the way she has, in all aspects of life.

"I thought...Seattle was the perfect solution," I murmur under my breath.

"For you, or for her?" Jules says quietly, matching my low tone.

I furrow my brow and glance at her. "For both of us. I...I love her. I fucking love her, Jules. I only want what's best for her. But it wasn't my place, I guess. I apologized but..." My words come out garbled as my throat tightens and my heart pounds in my ears. I can't lose her. I have to figure this out.

"I know you do love her," Rider says quietly. "It's easy to tell she loves you too, Wes. But something happened tonight, something frightened her."

I scoff, anger surging inside me. "Yeah, right into Sam's arms."

"Do you really think so, or is that old insecurities coming back to bite you in the ass?" Rider asks pointedly.

I blink, and try to remember exactly what was said tonight, but my goddamn brain is a hot mess. "What are you trying to say?"

"Do you really think, after everything that happened, that Charlie is going to walk away from you, and go for Sam?"

"She said they were friends. She said he called her Charlotte and...I guess not. She's not like that. She's not the kind of girl to go after bigger and better, like Breton. She's not even looking for a way out of here, not really." No, she's not like that at all. She's sweet and kind and loyal and smart, and driven, and...she's a daughter who wants to do right by her mother, but I know she doesn't belong in Toronto, which was why I did what I did. Not that she belongs in Seattle either, but she's driven to show her mother who she really is and what she really wants, by experiencing more.

"She said she didn't know who I was? I thought she knew I was a simple farm boy who was good at hockey. I thought...I thought she liked that guy. Was I wrong?"

"You're not. She likes that guy, Wes. But maybe tonight, what-ever was said, made her think you were that NHL player who had a harem of women, and that you wanted to make her into one of them, with the right clothes...name...job."

My heart somersaults in my chest as sweat breaks out on my skin. "Fuck." I go still and work to quiet my mind as my synapses fire at dangerous speeds. "Jesus, you're right. I called her Charlotte. I bought her a dress. I arranged a job interview in my hometown. When I apologized...I was apologizing for the job—thought I'd overstepped—but maybe she thought I was apologizing for trying to change her...and the fact that I did apologize was proof that I was trying to make her into Breton, or a bunny. Now it makes sense." I exhale harshly. "Shit."

My friends fall silent as I puzzle things out, and a boat engine has me lifting my head, searching for the woman I'm in love with.

"You would never do that," Jules says quietly.

"No, but I can see why she thought I was trying to change her, that I didn't know who she was..." I put my hand over my heart. "But I know who she is in here." I tug on the collar of my shirt, even though it's not the fabric constricting my breathing. It's the thoughts of losing Charlie. "She never let me finish explaining and jumped to conclusions, and I know why. I know exactly why she did that."

When it comes right to the heart of the matter, Charlie is afraid of losing herself, of following in her mother's footsteps only to end up alone. She said she never met anyone who wanted the same things as her, but she was wrong. I'm that man. I want what she wants, but went about it in ways that scared her, ways that made her think I was making her into something she wasn't, something that fit the vision of the NHL player—not the simple farm boy.

I am such a dense asshole.

Jules touches my arm, brings my attention back to her. "You two need to talk."

I take a deep breath of the heavy night air, smoke from the fireworks thick on my tongue. "How will I ever make her listen to me?"

"I don't know, but you better figure it out," Rider says.

"Maybe I can get her on the boat," Jules says. "And you can take her to the middle of the ocean where she has no choice but to listen."

"I don't want to trick her into anything. I want to be completely honest."

"Yeah, you're right and she'll probably dive in and swim to shore," Jules says, nodding her head like she's envisioning it.

"That's true," Rider agrees. "She's a woman who knows her own mind, that's for sure. But she's also a woman in love, so this needs to be fixed."

I go quiet, my heart aching to be with the woman I'm in love with. What the hell can I do to prove to her that I love her, that I know her and care about her and only have her best interests at heart? Voices boom behind us on the street, Digby Day's grand marshal's voice louder than the rest as he rings his bell, and that's when an idea hits harder than a runaway puck.

"I know what to do."

CHARLIE

I glance up from the scallop shucking demonstration to see Jules coming my way. My heart hammers and I blink my tired eyes—compliments of a sleepless night—to see if it's really her or if I'm seeing things. I honestly don't know what to expect. Will she be upset that I stormed out on Wes, or will she understand what happened? Does it matter? It's not like I'll see her again after today and the only reason I'm sitting at this table is because I made a commitment, even though I'm sure I'm the talk of the town today.

"Hi," she says and smiles as she stands across the table from me, bracing her hands on the back of the chair.

"Hi Jules."

Her smile is warm, and some of the tension inside me eases. "I'm here for the shucking demonstration."

I gesture toward the chair in front of her. "Have a seat."

She pulls the chair out and sits in it, leaning forward to examine the scallops. "Okay, so how do we do this?"

I pick up a scallop, stare at it, then drop it again. "Do you really want to do this?"

She crinkles her nose. "I actually just wanted to see how you were doing."

I exhale, and my stupid chin begins to quiver as my pulse pounds at the base of my throat. "I'm okay." It's a lie. I'm not okay. I'm not sure I'll ever be okay again. "How is Wes?" God, what am I doing? I don't know, but despite everything, I want to talk about him. Want to hear his name on my tongue, want to remember every minute with him.

"He's not so great."

I swallow. "Sorry. He's your friend and I..." I have no idea what to say. I reacted strongly last night after he told me about the job. Did I overreact? I want to be with him. There's no question about that. But everything he was saying frightened me. I can't love and lose him. I can't follow in my mother's footsteps, only to end up alone and broken-hearted. Not with Wes. It would kill me.

"He's hurting."

"I'm sorry," I say again.

"You're hurting," she says quietly.

I press my hands to my face. I don't want her to see my tears. "It's complicated, Jules." I am not going to drag her into our problems, and I have no idea what Wes said about me, or what happened last night after I left. But if he wanted to keep things private, and he's a private guy, I'm not about to talk about him behind his back. "You should probably go hang out with him. I know you're not here much longer."

She sits there for a second, like she's debating her next move. "Can I ask one question, and can you answer honestly?"

I frown. "Jules…"

"Do you love him?"

A ridiculous sound climbs out of my throat and a few people glance at me. God, I don't like being the center of attention any more than Wes does.

"Wait, don't answer that. I already know you do, so I don't want to waste my one question on something I already know."

I stare at her. She knows I love Wes? I almost laugh. I guess it's pretty obvious to anyone who spent time with us.

"Do you really think Wes was trying to change you into something you're not?"

"He apologized for it, so yeah, I guess so."

"Please, Charlie. Think about it." I open my mouth and she holds her hand up to stop me. "Take a minute. Please. Think about who he really is." She puts her hand over her heart. "In here."

I close my eyes as a seagull squawks overhead and I drown out the din of the crowd around us as my mind travels back to the first time I met Wes, right up until last night. He's always been kind to me, and always made me feel good about myself and my skills. He teased about loving my rubber boots, admired me fully when I was in my coveralls. Never once did he make fun of me, or make me feel anything less than a woman. He was determined to give me a vacation on Brier Island, wanting to do things for me. No man has ever done that before, and the sex…ohmigod, the sex.

He touched me with such care, worshipped me with his eyes, his hands, his mouth and his cock. I swallow as a fine shiver goes through me. Would a man like that want to make me into something different, when he seemed to like me because of my differences?

My lids fly open and I find Jules watching me carefully.

"Jules," I say, my voice tight.

"He's a good guy, Charlie."

"I thought...he wasn't?"

"No, he wasn't, and he was apologizing because he thought he overstepped, trying to get you a job in Seattle."

I glance into the crowd, anxiousness welling up inside me. "Why did he do that, though? Why would he want me to move away from everything I love?"

You love him.

I glance at the people milling about. "This is my home."

Is it really even home without Wes here?

Jules gives me a gentle smile. "I think there's more to it, Charlie."

"What do you mean?"

She stands. "Why don't we go find out?"

I sit there for a long moment, nearly paralyzed as I sort through the fog clouding my thoughts. I shake my head hard enough to clear the haze and rattle some sense back into my flustered brain. As the world around me settles and rights itself, I think about Wes, and every moment we spent together and that's when I realize what's important and what isn't.

Wes is important, and so is what he wants!

I love him and I also trust him, which means where we live doesn't matter, because I won't be sad and miserable if I leave here—with him. He's also not my father—he's not going to hurt me and leave me broken—and I'm not my mother, unwilling to compromise for love, not when it's with the right man. The truth is, I can always come back here to visit. The sea is in my soul, but the sea isn't going anywhere, and Wes is more important to me than any of that anyways.

A gasp crawls out of my throat. My God, I messed things up horribly.

"Jules," I cry out, as my gaze flies to her. "I hurt him. I accused him of things. He'll probably never talk to me again."

"Then maybe you should just listen." Having no idea what she's talking about, I let her link her arm through mine and drag me through the busy streets. "Where are we going? The parade is about to start and I don't want to get caught in the middle of it."

"The middle of it is exactly where you need to be."

"What are you…" I glance up and take in the first float sailing down the street. It's a lobster boat on wheels, and Wes is standing on the deck. "Oh my God. What is he doing?"

Jules has a big smile on her face, as she holds me tight, like she's afraid I'm going to run away. The crowd cheers as he speaks into the microphone, to test it. "Why is he up there? He hates crowds like this, and he hates being the center of attention."

"I know."

"Jules?"

"Time to listen, my friend."

I turn back to Wes and my heart squeezes as I take in his handsome face, no ball cap to conceal his identity. He's dressed in the same jeans he was wearing when I surprised him on the farm, and he's in a T-shirt that showcases hard, homegrown muscles. My hand itches to touch him again, as he comes closer. My God, I love him. I love him so much. But I let my fears come between us.

"Charlie," he says into the microphone as he points to me, and the entire crowd turns my way. Heat floods my face, and when my knees go weak, Rider comes up on the other side of me, and puts his arm around me.

"Hey Charlie," he says.

Panic grips my chest. "What's going on?"

He doesn't tell me, instead he stares up at Wes as he makes a spectacle of himself.

"For those of you in the crowd who don't know Charlie, let me tell you, she's the kindest sweetest, smartest fisherman, or rather fisherwoman, I know. She wears coveralls that drive me insane, and rubber boots that put heels to shame. This is her hometown, where she was born, grew up and wants to spend the rest of her life. I get that."

He does get that. I never should have questioned it. I glance around, and spot my mother and sisters in the crowd. They're watching me with big smiles on their faces.

"Her name is Charlotte, but my cousin." He scans the crowd. "He's around here somewhere. He decided to call her Charlie, and the name stuck. While I love the name, I made a mistake and thought she'd prefer to go by Charlotte. I thought I was righting a wrong from the past." He winks at the crowd and they go crazy. "A rookie mistake."

"I made a mistake too," I blurt out without thinking, and as all eyes turn to me, shocked at my outburst, I almost back away, but no, this is important. Wes is important and if he's going to stand up there in front of this crowd and open himself up, I am too. The float stops in front of me.

Wes angles his head, his eyes dark and serious...yet full of hope. "Charlie?"

"I made a mistake, Wes. When I told you I didn't know who you were."

His head drops, and his shoulder's sag like they're no longer carrying the weight of the world. "Who am I, Charlie?"

"You're a farm boy who is good at hockey."

A slow smile curls his lips. "That's right. That's exactly who I am, Charlie. At heart that's who I am."

"It's that boy I fell in love with."

He goes still, and gasps sound in the crowd. "You...love me?"

"Of course I love you."

The crowd starts clapping, and Wes jumps from the float, and people part to give him a path to me. He stops in front of me, and tears flood my eyes.

"I love you too, Charlie. The job in Seattle. It's part time. You said I didn't know you, but I do. This job, it's seasonal, and you'd have your summers back here, where you belong. You can experience other things in Seattle, like you want, like your Mom wants, but every year, we can come back here. You can keep running your tour business, and I want to do it with you. I want to spend all my time with you. Of course, I still want to get a cottage on Watauga beach. Jules will kill me if I don't, and I think you'll like it there, and you'll like my teammates and their wives." Without taking a breath, he continues with. "I want to be your partner in life. I want what you want. I want you happy. I want to knit our kids toques and sweaters." He's about to continue, but I put my fingers to his lips, to hush him as my heart practically pounds out of my chest.

"Wes. I want all those things, and I want them with you, and no one else." I blink through the tears welling up in my eyes. "When you bought the dress, called me Charlotte, got me a job that took me away from here...I thought you were trying to make me into something else. I saw what happened to my parents and I was afraid. But we're not them, and I should have listened, should have let you explain. That's on me, not you. It was a rookie mistake on my part, and I want you to know, I'm not afraid anymore." I put my hands on his face. "What you want is important to me too, Wes, and home is wherever we are...together. Before I heard a word you had to say to me today, I had already concluded that I'd go anywhere with you. We don't have to be here to be together and happy."

His throat makes a sound as he swallows, and his chest rises and falls fast. "You mean that?"

"Yes."

"That means a lot to me, but the sea is in your soul, Charlie, I'd never take—"

I press my lips to his, to smother his words and the crowd cheers. "You don't have to explain anything else to me," I whisper. "I get it. You know me, just like I know you."

"I do have one thing to explain." His look is sheepish when he says, "It's a confession, really."

My heart stalls. "A confession?"

"Yeah, you see, I wasn't honest with you. Not totally."

I falter a little but he puts his arms around me to hold me to his body. "When you asked if faking it with you, if kissing you, was all to prove to Breton I was taken...it wasn't the entire truth."

I frown, not understanding. "Wes?"

"I kissed you because I wanted to. Needed to. I think the second I set eyes on you at the shop I fell in love."

"You thought I was a guy."

His laugh curls around me. "God, you're never going to let me live that down are you, Mack," he teases as Jules and Rider smile as they hug each other.

"How about we go somewhere..." I go up on my toes to kiss him and whisper in his ear. "Somewhere private so I can show you that I'm all girl, and we can start planning those toques and sweaters you want to knit."

He smiles at me and my heart soars when he picks me up and spins me around. "I love you, Charlie."

I grab his hand and tug. "Then come on, farm boy who's good at hockey. Come show me how much."

EPILOGUE

Wes

One Year Later:

After a very successful NHL season, Charlie and I are happy to be back in rural Nova Scotia, headed to Brier Island, with Rider, Jules and Sophie, who is now almost two. They're not just here for whale watching. Nope, Rider is standing up for me next week, and Jules is standing up for Charlie. If it was left to me, we would have been married last year, right after I told her I loved her, but she wanted to wait and do it right.

As we walk along the dock, Charlie, Jules and little Sophie ahead of us, I glance at my buddy Rider, who has far too many bags over his shoulder, and ask, "Did I ever thank you for letting me know the team was looking to hire a part time manager?"

He laughs and slaps me on the back. "Only about a million times." Charlie glances at me over her shoulder and when she gives me a little smile and bites her bottom lip—our secret message—I stifle a groan. My heart squeezes. I love seeing her this happy, and she jumped right into her job with both feet, and our manager raves about Charlie's skills.

All the wives and players naturally took her in, and she's a part of our big family now, but her family is and always will be here, which is why it was so important for me that we return every summer. We went ahead and bought a cottage on Watauga Beach. Charlie fell in love with one big enough for a family of ten, and believe me, I'm working on that. Although there is a part of me that's a bit worried that we're not pregnant by now. Although I've kept that worry to myself.

We reach the fishing boat, and Charlie drops to her knees to talk to Sophie, telling her all about the whales. Sophie giggles and claps her hands, and my heart fills with all the love I have for Charlie, all the love I can't wait to give our own kids.

Charlie jumps onto the boat with grace and helps Jules and Sophie on. I follow behind and Rider tosses me a few of his bags.

"How much stuff do you need, Jules?" I ask.

She lifts her chin an inch. "When you have your own child, you'll understand."

I grin, but again, my stomach tightens. Maybe I should get my swimmers checked?

"Okay, let's get a life jacket on Sophie, and everyone sit while I get us out of the bay."

Everyone does as she asks, and I can't help but follow her to the cabin and watch as she effortlessly maneuvers the big boat out to deeper water.

"Impressive," I say, and Charlie glances at me over her shoulder.

"If you don't sit and follow the rules while I'm piloting this boat, I'll make you wear a life jacket."

I laugh as we go back to our first time on the boat, and recite the same words. "Can I sit in here?" I ask, as I glance at the bench.

"Fine, as long as you don't distract me. I need to get out to open water without running into any other vessels."

I sit, and can't take my eyes off my beautiful fiancée, soon to be bride. I let my gaze fall over her, take in the small smile permanently on her face. As I study her, I note some small changes. The slight flush of her cheeks, the thickness of her hair, the new plumpness in her body. Seattle has been good for her, for both of us.

"Now that Jules and Rider know Brier Island, does that mean they can tour on their own, so I can keep you in the dome all to myself, all weekend?"

She grins. "You know it's all about customer experience, Wes."

"And you know what this customer wants to experience, right?" I stand, and step up behind her. Unable to keep my hands to myself, I slide them around her body, and cup her breasts, take in their fullness.

"We're about to get married. I don't think that qualifies you as a guest anymore, but I think there are special provisions for husbands."

She glances at me over her shoulder, and my heart swells. "I love you so much, Charlie."

"I love…" her words fall off, and her body goes completely still.

"Charlie?" I move to the side to see her face. "You've lost your sea legs," I tease, but my smile falls when she pales, puts her hand over her mouth, and backs up. I quickly take control of the boat and slow it down when she darts from the cabin.

"Charlie are you okay?" Jules asks, and I stop the boat and run to Charlie's aid. I find her bent over the side of the boat, ill.

I hold her hair back as she empties her stomach, and worry zings through me. She hasn't been on a boat in a while. But I wouldn't think someone as seasoned as her would get seasick upon returning.

"Where's your bag?" I ask, and run my hand along her back. "I'll get you some Dramamine."

She shakes her head no, and I glance at a very worried Jules and Rider. "Can you grab us a bottle of water?"

Rider comes back with the water and I open it. Charlie takes a big drink, and rinses her mouth. She sits on the bench and wipes the moisture from her brow. When she realizes we're all watching, she frowns.

"I'm sorry."

"Don't be sorry." I press my hand to her forehead. "You're sick."

I glance at Jules, who is a nurse. "Do you want to check her temperature?"

"No need," Jules says a slight grin on her face, like she suddenly knows something I don't. I mean, I know I can be dense at times, but I'm really worried about Charlie here. Why won't she check her temperature?

"We need to turn back."

I'm about to stand, and turn the boat around, when a hand on my arms stops me. "No, Wes."

She pulls me closer, and holds my hands. "I wanted to wait until we got to Brier Island to tell you, but I guess the cat's out of the bag…" She laughs. "So to speak."

"I'm lost, babe."

"We're pregnant Wes."

The world stops moving around me, and I'm sure the sea just went completely calm as I stare at my beautiful fiancée, her words pinging around inside my brain. My heart suddenly speeds up, and the world begins moving again as I absorb and digest her words.

"We're…pregnant?"

Her smile is wide, and her eyes are sparkling as she nods.

"We're pregnant!" I shout, and jump up, pulling her with me. I throw my arms around her and start spinning her, but that's when I realize that might not be a good idea. I set her down. "I'm sorry," I say quickly. "Did I make you sick again?"

"It's okay. I feel better."

I drop to my knees, and press my lips to her stomach. "Hi baby."

"Baby," Sophie says, and we all start laughing. Jules and Rider stand to give us hugs and congratulations and tears fall down my cheeks as I hug my little family, which is about to get bigger and bigger if I have anything to do with it.

"Whale," Jules says.

"Hey, I'm not that big yet," Charlie teases and they both laugh as a whale comes close to the boat, breaches, and showers us all with good luck, but I'm already the luckiest man on the face of the planet.

"I love you, Charlie."

"I love you too, Weston."

"Why did you just call me that?"

She rubs her belly. "Trying it out, in case we have a boy."

My heart swells so much I fear it's going to explode. "How did I ever get so lucky?"

She goes on tiptoes to whisper in my ear. "Lucky? Yeah, you're going to get lucky, farm boy. Just as soon as I get you alone in the dome."

* * *

Thank you so much for reading, **The Rookie**, book 10 in my **Players on Ice**. I hope you loved this story as much as I loved writing it. Keep reading for an excerpt of **The Sweet Talker**, book 11!

The Sweet Talker

Brody

Six days until Christmas Eve:

"Why do I feel like I just drove straight onto the set of a Hallmark movie?" I ask my buddy Declan as I look through my dirty windshield and take in the decked-out shops lining Main Street. Thank God I don't have epilepsy. All the flashing lights in the store windows, not to mention the sparkling spruce wreaths hanging from every lamppost, are liable to trigger a damn seizure.

I slow my sports car on the slushy streets of Holiday Peak, Massachusetts, the sugary sweet town Declan calls home. Talk about a community taking Christmas to the extreme, and no, I'm not secretly enjoying the festive energy bubbling up around me. Not much, anyway.

"Watch a lot of Hallmark movies, do you?" Declan asks, busting my balls, and why wouldn't he? Do you know any guys that blurt shit out about Hallmark movies, like they're totally into them? Didn't think so.

I glance at my buddy as he stares out the window, nostalgia all over his face. Declan and I became close when I joined the Seattle Shooters defensive line up a couple of years ago. He took me under his wing, and we've been tight ever since. While he knows a lot about me, more than most, he doesn't need to know I'm a sucker for a good Christmas movie, which undoubtedly stems from far too many craptastic Christmases over the years.

He tears his gaze from the festive streets, and his brow arches in challenge as he waits for me to answer. "So that's a yes? You watch a lot of Hallmark movies?"

"Sometimes I'm too lazy to stretch for the remote," I say, rubbing my eyes. The drive from my place in Boston to Declan's hometown isn't a long one. I'm just tired from kicking ass during our winning game against Detroit two nights ago and I'm damn well looking forward to this break.

"Which means you were already watching the Women's Network, correct?" He grins. "Look I don't care, just stop denying it."

I shake my head. Leave it to Declan to call me on my shit. Every. Single. Time. I lift my chin. "You don't know my life," I shoot back. I hide a grin and add, "Sometimes those movies are on the Lifetime channel, you know." We both laugh at that. Yeah, I get it. Hours spent watching chick flicks hardly fits my image, and it's best that information doesn't leave this car. While I might be known as the Sweet Talker—and I'm not being cocky when I say this, but I'm pretty good at scoring with the ladies—on the ice, I'm a pit bull with one job: keep the opponents from scoring. But enough of that. I need a change of subject before Declan makes me cash in my man card.

"Do I really have to bring a date to Christmas Eve dinner?" I ask with a groan as I sink deeper into the driver's seat. To be honest, I'm a little played out, and agreed to join Declan for Christmas because he grew up in a sleepy town with a nearby ski hill, and I need downtime. That, and my father, an NHL hall of famer, couldn't care less about seeing his kid over the holidays. He's too busy with wife number five, or maybe it's six, and don't even get me started on my biological mother. But sometimes I think I worked so hard at hockey just to get his attention, his approval. You'd think he'd be proud of his son following in his footsteps. I guess he's too self-centered and interested in his own pleasures to care.

Declan shrugs. "Up to you, but like I said, no one sits alone at Mom's table. If the chair next to you is empty, she'll fill it with my cousin Eugenie, and that woman…" He gives a low slow whistle. "Let's just say she's a huge Brody Tucker fan, and I'm pretty sure she wants you to be her baby daddy."

I laugh out loud, holding one hand up. "I draw the line there, bro."

"I know you do, so you better put a plan together and find someone to fill that chair, before Mom does and you find out you're Houdini Eugenie's baby daddy before you even realize you've been unzipped."

"Note to self, steer clear of Houdini Eugenie." Snow starts falling again, and I turn on my wipers, spreading a streak of dirty slush across my window. Way to mess up my visibility. I scrunch to look through a clean streak. "Where am I going to find a date this late, anyway?"

"You have six days."

I consider that for a moment. "I guess that's plenty of time to sweet talk a girl into a fancy dinner at your parents' place." Declan snorts, shaking his head. "What?" I ask.

"Maybe the women in Holiday Peak won't fall for your charm." He taps his head. "They're kind of smart like that around these parts."

I tap the steering wheel and grin. "Guess I won't know if I don't try."

"Just don't try it with Nikki," he says, a warning in his voice. "I don't want her getting mixed up with the likes of you."

"You're the one they call Heartbreaker, not me, and it's not like you have any claim on her. All you do is hang out when you're home and then return to the team in a shit mood. If you like her, do something about it."

"It's not like that." He exhales, averting my gaze, but not before I catch the frown on his forehead. I'm not exactly sure what the deal is with him and Nikki. I guess I'll never know because he shuts down whenever her name comes up.

"Who should I ask, then?" I scan the sidewalk, looking for possible candidates. A pretty brunette walks by and I perk up, until I notice the little boy by her side. Nope. Not her. Moving along. It's not that I have anything against kids. Simply put, relationships never work out for me, and no way do I want to drag a kid into my world only to screw him up when I eventually screw up. I don't want to be the cause of anyone's therapy. He's better off never having known me on a personal level.

Declan pulls his phone from his pocket and sends a text. He seems a bit distracted when he says, "Are you suggesting I pick someone for you?"

"This is your town, isn't it? You know the women better than I do, and maybe Nikki has a friend. Just point the way." I offer him my best smile. "I'll take care of the rest."

"Let me get this straight. You're saying whoever I pick, you can charm to the table?"

"Is that a challenge?"

He stares at his phone for a second, shoves it into his pocket and looks at me. "Maybe."

I toss him a cocky grin. Being a star in the NHL comes with its perks—Declan knows that firsthand. You know what being a star in the NHL doesn't come with? Long term relationships. At least not for me. Lots of my buddies have fallen in love and are now married with kids. But the only thing I know about love is how to mess it up, which is why I no longer try.

"Try me, bro. Pick a girl and I'll get her to the table." I flick on the windshield washer, but no fluid comes out. "I can't see a thing."

"Wait, pull over."

"What?"

"Right here," he practically shouts. "Stop the car."

I jerk the car to the right, and my suspension squeals as my front right tire plunges into a slush covered pothole near the curb. The god-awful screeching sound is followed by a gasp so loud it drowns out the song on the radio. My heart jumps into my throat. "What the hell?"

"Oh, shit." Declan jerks his thumb to the right. "You just soaked someone."

Worry races through me as I kill the ignition and jump from the car. Circling the front, my eyes go wide when my gaze lands on a girl around my age—late twenties. It's a bit hard to tell exactly how old she is as she stands there gasping for air, cold, wet slushy snow dripping from her—compliments of my erratic driving.

"I'm so sorry," I blurt out, thankful that I hadn't done more damage, like actually hit her. "Declan, grab me something." As Declan goes to the trunk, I take in the woman trying to catch her breath as she swipes wet, dirty snow from her face. I scan the length of her. Christ, I don't think there's an inch of her that I missed. "I'm so sorry," I say again. "Let me help you."

"No thanks. I think you've done enough already," she shoots back, a cold shiver wracking her body. Okay, she's upset because I soaked her. I can understand that, and maybe she was headed somewhere important, and needed to be, well... dry. Despite her protest, I take my coat off and hold it out to her as Declan comes back with one of our team towels. He spreads it open, and she takes the towel and wipes her face. "Thank you," she says quietly to Declan.

"Here, take my coat," I say.

She hands the towel back to Declan, shaking her head at me. "I'm fine."

Clearly, she's not fine, but I'm not about to call her on that as she averts my gaze and scans the snowbank. "Let me make it up to you." I reach for my wallet. "I'll pay for the dry cleaning."

She holds her hand out, palm facing me. "I don't want your money."

"Please, let me do something to make this up to you. Dinner? New clothes?" She toys with the zipper on her winter jacket. "Axe throwing?" I glance up and down the streets. Maybe they don't have that here.

Her head lifts and she glares at me like I might have just escaped an institution. Maybe under the circumstances, with her soaked and freezing, I can understand how axe throwing was a little bit out there.

"Keep the money." She wrings out her ponytail, and that's when I notice the pretty green flecks in her dark brown eyes. "Maybe you could use it for driving lessons."

I bite back a wince as Declan stifles a chuckle. She looks down again, searches the snowbank. A thunderous noise rumbles down the street and I jump back, pulling my new friend—or rather enemy—with me, before the snowplow soaks us both. The plow drops its blade at the front of my car and scrapes up the snow.

"Great," she says under her breath, and I examine the layer of packed snow with her, even though I have no idea what it is I'm looking for.

"Did you lose something?"

She briefly closes her eyes, like she's trying to convince herself murder is wrong, and then says, "No, I just like to search snowbanks for fun. It's a pasttime here in Holiday

Peak, something you out of towners wouldn't know anything about."

"How do you know I'm from out of town?"

She arches a brow glancing at my sports car, which isn't ideal for this mountainous town. *Alrighty then.* People on the street slow as they see us, a few pointing at Declan and me with recognition. "Can I drop you somewhere?" I gesture toward my car.

"No."

"Maybe you could call someone to pick you up. Do you have a boyfriend or husband I could call?"

I'm not hitting on her—I don't think. It's just that she looks a bit traumatized, and might need someone other than me coming to her rescue.

"No."

I really don't know why my chest loosened at that answer. We're different people from different worlds, and yeah, I can't forget her instant dislike of me, and maybe even my car.

"You should probably get inside before you freeze to death," I suggest.

Her head lifts. Speaking of death... As her murderous eyes turn on me, I'm pretty sure she's thinking about ways to bury me in the slushy snow, or maybe she's reconsidering the axe throwing, with me as her target. "You think?" she shoots back.

Clearly, we're off to a good start.

"I'm sorry. Look. Can we start again?"

"You can keep the towel," Declan says, holding it out for her. She looks at the Seattle Shooters emblem, and her eyes lift. She smiles for the first time, and my heart stills a little in my chest. Jesus, she's gorgeous—when she's not contemplating killing me, that is. "Declan Bradbury. I've heard a lot about you. You're famous in this town, and it's nice to meet you in person."

"Nice to meet you too, and you are...?"

"Freezing to death. Thanks to your friend." She searches the snow again, and her teeth clatter a little louder.

I step closer, crowd her, wanting to offer her my warmth but afraid of getting a knee to the nuts. As I crowd her, I breathe in her delicious scent. Cookies and cream and...chocolate. Not just any chocolate. No, she smells like the expensive kind my third stepmother used to put out at Christmas—before she disappeared from my life, taking a little bit of my heart with her.

"I can help you find whatever it is you're looking for," I offer.

She stares at the plow as it takes a turn, and for a second I think she might cry. But the anger is back in her eyes when she turns to me. "I don't...need your help...you've..." Choppy words through clattering teeth fall off as a shop door opens behind her, a little bell ringing to alert the staff to a customer.

"Done enough, I know." Feeling like total crap, I adjust my ballcap as she turns, disappearing into the shop. The delectable scent of warm gooey chocolate fills the street, as the door falls shut behind her.

I stand there for a moment, a little confused at her sudden departure. Then again, it's possible she was on the brink of hypothermia. I put my jacket back on, reading the sign above the door: The Chocolate Lab. I guess she must work there.

"You been here five whole minutes, and look at you, making friends," Declan says.

I turn to my buddy, and shrug. "Who the hell was that, anyway?

He looks past my shoulders up and down the street. "I don't know."

"Don't you know everyone in this town?"

"She must be new around here. That shop wasn't here last time I was home."

His mouth turns up at the corner, presenting me with those double dimples that drive women wild. "Axe throwing?"

"Cut me some slack, I panicked, and what the hell is the matter with you? Why are you smiling like the village idiot?"

"Because I pick her." He points to the chocolate shop. "She's the girl you have to charm to the dinner table."

I scoff. "Oh, hell no. She's a man-hater."

"I don't know if I'd say that. I thought she was rather sweet." My jaw drops and he continues with, "She knew who I was and smiled at me."

"Then you date her."

He shoves his hands into his pockets, and rolls one shoulder. "No, I think I'll leave that to you."

I cover my crotch. "I'm kind of fond of these guys, Declan, and wouldn't mind them intact when I leave here after Christmas."

He laughs. "Then I guess you have your work cut out for you."

"My work cut out for me? No, my friend, getting her to the table isn't going to take work, it's going to take a Christmas miracle."

"Are you saying you can't do it? That the infamous Sweet Talker can't sweet talk his way into any woman's life?" He turns and heads down the street, stopping outside a coffee shop.

I make a move to go when my foot knocks something loose in the snow. I glanced down and spot something shiny lodged between the bank and a lamppost. I snatch the object up, and the second I realize what I'm holding, a wide smile crosses my face.

"Not saying that at all," I shoot back.

He pulls open the coffee shop door, pausing to look back at me. "Then it's on?"

I grin, as I shove my ticket to winning this challenge into my pocket. "It's already done."

* * *

If you want to see what kind of trouble Josie and Brody get into, check it out here **The Sweet Talker**

The Puck Charmer

The Troublemaker

The Rule Breaker

The Rookie

The Sweet Talker

In the Line of Duty

His Obsession Next Door

His Strings to Pull

His Trouble in Talulah

His Taste of Temptation

His Moment to Steal

His Best Friend's Girl

His Reason to Stay

Confessions

Confessions of a Bad Boy Professor

Confessions of a Bad Boy Officer

Confessions of a Bad Boy Fighter

Confessions of a Bad Boy Doctor

Confessions of a Bad Boy Gamer

Confessions of a Bad Boy Millionaire

Confessions of a Bad Boy Santa

Confessions of a Bad Boy CEO

Hands On

Hands On

Body Contact

Full Exposure

Dossier

Private Reserve

House Rules

Under Pressure

Big Catch

Brazilian Fantasy

Improper Proposal

Boys of Beachville

Good at Being Bad

Igniting the Bad Boy

Bad Girl Therapy

Stone Cliff Series:

Crashing Down

Wasted Summer

Love Lessons

Wrapped Up

Eternal Pleasure Series

Instinctive

Impulsive

Indulgent

Sun Stroked Series

Seaside Seduction

Deep Desire

Private Pleasure

Captured and Claimed Series:

Yours to Take

Yours to Teach

Yours to Keep

Firefighter Heat Series

Fever

Siren

Flash Fire

Playing For Keeps Series

Slow Ride

Wild Ride

Sweet Ride

Breaking the Rules:

Hold Me Down Hard

Pin Me Up Proper

Tie Me Down Tight

Stand Alone Title:

Hands on with the CEO

Torn Between Two Brothers

Holiday Spirit

Unleashed

Knocking on Demon's Door

Web of Desire

ABOUT CATHRYN

New York Times and *USA today* Bestselling author, Cathryn is a wife, mom, sister, daughter, and friend. She loves dogs, sunny weather, anything chocolate (she never says no to a brownie) pizza and red wine. She has two teenagers who keep her busy with their never ending activities, and a husband who is convinced he can turn her into a mixed martial arts fan. Cathryn can never find balance in her life, is always trying to find time to go to the gym, can never keep up with emails, Facebook or Twitter and tries to write page-turning books that her readers will love.

Connect with Cathryn:
Newsletter https://app.mailerlite.com/webforms/landing/c1f8n1
Twitter: https://twitter.com/writercatfox
Facebook: https://www.facebook.com/AuthorCathrynFox?ref=hl
Blog: http://cathrynfox.com/blog/
Goodreads: https://www.goodreads.com/author/show/91799.Cathryn_Fox

Pinterest http://www.pinterest.com/catkalen/